Y0-BWT-580

54

CALGARY PUBLIC LIBRARY

Death Mask

ALSO BY HUGH PENTECOST

MACLEOD BRANCH

Death Mask

Hugh Pentecost

A Red Badge Novel of Suspense

DODD, MEAD & COMPANY
New York

Copyright © 1980 by Judson Philips
All rights reserved
No part of this book may be reproduced in any form
without permission in writing from the publisher
Printed in the United States of America

1 2 3 4 5 6 7 8 9 10

Library of Congress Cataloging in Publication Data

Philips, Judson Pentecost, 1903–
    Death mask.

    (A Red badge novel of suspense)
    I. Title.
PZ3.P5412Dd   [PS3531.H442]   813'.52   80–15717
ISBN 0–396–07883–4

PART ONE

1

The murder of a doctor and his nurse in the doctor's office in the Murray Hill section of New York City would not ordinarily have made headlines. We are living in a time of terror and violence. A huge metropolis like New York is said to be swarming with drug addicts who would think nothing of breaking into a doctor's office and killing whoever stood in the way of their stealing narcotics they had to have. The night Dr. Claude Martine and his nurse, one Julia Prentiss, were shot to death the whole world was in turmoil. Fifty Americans were in their seventy-ninth day of being held hostage in Iran by so-called "students." The Russians had invaded Afghanistan, and the dread specter of World War III was in the back of people's minds. If anything more was needed to distract attention from the murder of a doctor and his nurse on Murray Hill, it was a political year. Primaries in thirty-five states to nominate candidates for president of the United States in the two major parties were about to get under way. On that particular night the press, radio, and television were poised to tell the country the returns from one of the first of those primaries, in Iowa. The incumbent president had two major rivals in his own party, and six or eight prominent figures were slugging it out for first place in the opposite party. Dr. Martine and Julia Prentiss would have been specks of dust in the public eye except for one fact. The murdered bodies of the doctor and his nurse were discovered and reported to the police by a man in the political spotlight in the State of New York.

Bartley J. Craven, Bart to his friends and the general public, was expected to announce that he was a candidate for a seat in the United States Senate. The incumbent senator, a man in his seventies, had not yet announced whether he would or would not run again. That announcement was imminent. If the senator were not going to run again, then it was pretty generally known that Bart Craven would be ready to throw his hat in the ring and campaign, full steam ahead, for the office. Bart Craven was well qualified. He had served in the State Department, he had been a special envoy to the Middle East in times of crisis, he had been a close advisor to two presidents. His record was marred by only one flaw. Seven years ago he had been a central figure in a tragedy with overtones of mystery. The public doesn't like political candidates with unsolved mysteries in their lives. Involvement in a second sensation, a double murder, unless he was instantly cleared of any complicity, was not likely to enhance his political chances.

Bart Craven had one piece of luck going his way on the night he discovered the bodies of the murdered doctor and his nurse on Murray Hill. The Homicide man who came to the scene was Lieutenant Mark Kreevich, who was, it just happened, a close friend of a man who was expected to play an important role in

Craven's campaign—if and when. The result was that Craven got kid-glove treatment in the early going.

Julian Quist Associates, located in a finger of glass and steel that points to the sky in the Grand Central Station area, is, perhaps, the top public relations firm in the country. Julian Quist, tall, slender, blond, with a profile that could have belonged to a Greek Apollo carved on an old coin, a flamboyant dresser, attracts as much attention in public places as a movie star. His professional and personal lives get constant attention from the lady gossip columnists. Most of them have, however, long ago given up making sly remarks about the fact that Lydia Morton, a dark and beautiful lady, shares a duplex apartment on Beekman Place with Quist. Lydia Morton is a writer and researcher for Julian Quist Associates, and she and Quist belong to each other. Their relationship is more solid than most marriages. In a time when half the people who live together are not married, Julian Quist and Lydia Morton were the best possible advertisements for that way of life.

It was a few minutes after eleven on that January night when the phone rang on the little bar in the corner of Quist's living room. He was sitting on a bar stool, sipping a Jack Daniels on the rocks. Lydia was fussing at something in the kitchen just beyond. Quist picked up the phone. Only friends and business associates had the unlisted number.

"Julian? Mark Kreevich."

"Hi, chum," Quist said.

"I didn't get you up, did I? I want to talk."

"So talk."

"More than a phone conversation."

"Come over, then. Lydia and I were waiting up to hear about the Iowa primaries. There's a special broadcast at about eleven-thirty. Lydia's putting together a mushroom omelette. Shall she count you in?"

"If you think it goes with murder," Kreevich said. "Because that's what I want to talk about."

Kreevich is a dark, intense, steel spring of a man, with pale grey eyes that can occasionally darken when something amuses him. He is a new breed of cop, a man with a law degree, and a knowledge of all the modern techniques of criminal investigation. His and Quist's paths had crossed some time before when they had both been concerned with a murder case. Quist found himself working with a very tough professional who had, on the side, a taste for the arts, theater, music. The result was mutual respect and a warm friendship.

Kreevich arrived at Beekman Place about ten minutes after his call. He was crisp, almost cold. Quist recognized the signs of a man at work. Kreevich wanted no drink, but if there was coffee? Lydia, lovely in a wine-red housecoat, her dark hair hanging loose to her shoulders, brought him a mug from the kitchen. Rather absurdly, Kreevich commented on how mild the winter had been. He sipped his coffee and lit a cigarette. He was a chain smoker. Quist slid an ash tray down the bar to him and waited.

"About an hour and a half ago," Kreevich said finally, "a friend of yours walked into a doctor's office on East Thirty-eighth Street and found the doctor and his nurse shot to death."

"What friend?" Quist asked.

Lydia had paused in the doorway to the kitchen to listen.

"Bart Craven," Kreevich said.

Quist felt his jaw muscles tighten. "So?" he said.

6

"Craven behaved very properly," Kreevich said. "He says he had an appointment with Dr. Claude Martine. He walked in. That's the way it is at that office. You just walk into a waiting room. There's a receptionist during the regular daytime hours, but she'd long since gone home. It was exactly a quarter past nine, the time Craven had been given. He waited a few minutes and nobody showed. He called out the doctor's name. Nothing. He looked into the inner office. There he saw the doctor and his nurse sprawled out on the floor. Craven knows a gunshot wound when he sees one. Served in the army in Korea. The doctor and his nurse had both been shot in the forehead, right between the eyes."

"Weapon?" Quist asked.

"Nothing there. I don't have the medical examiner's report yet, but I suspect a small caliber handgun. Craven went back out into the waiting room, picked up the phone, using a handkerchief to keep from messing things up with his own fingerprints, and called the police. He waited. Patrol car cops came and then I came. He identified himself and of course I knew who he was, knew that he was a client of yours."

"So what's wrong with what he did?"

Kreevich's mouth moved in a tight smile. "What's wrong, I guess, is that he may have told me the truth. He opened up a can of peas."

"I don't follow," Quist said.

"I asked him how come an appointment at quarter past nine at night. Was he sick? What was the doctor treating him for? The doctor, he said, wasn't treating him for anything. He didn't know the doctor. Said he never heard of him until he got a phone call from him about eight-thirty. Dr. Claude Martine, on the phone, told Craven that if he'd come to his office on East

7

Thirty-eighth Street, he, the doctor, would tell Craven what happened to his wife seven years ago."

"Oh, brother!" Quist said.

"So, what did happen to his wife seven years ago?" Kreevich asked.

"It's a matter of record," Quist said.

"And I have a man at headquarters checking it out for me," Kreevich said. "It will probably take hours for him to dig up what you can tell me in ten minutes. You can also give me a thumbnail on Bart Craven."

"Is he in trouble?"

"I don't know, Julian. That's why I'm here."

Quist reached for the bottle of Jack Daniels and poured himself a fresh drink. He lifted his glass to the light, frowning, as if he hoped to see something in the amber-colored liquid that would help.

"Bart Craven isn't an old friend of mine," he told Kreevich. "As a matter of fact he is a relatively new client. You know I play squash at the Athletic Club? There's a pleasant guy there, about my speed although he's a little older, name of Jack Milburn. We play a couple of times a week. Five or six months ago he told me he had been associated all his life, socially and later in business, with Bart Craven. Craven was like his older brother, Jack told me. Craven had about made up his mind to run for the Senate if the present incumbent decided he'd had enough. If that happened, would Julian Quist Associates agree to mount a campaign for Craven? I asked why Craven needed a public relations firm in addition to the regular political workers."

"The disappearance of his wife seven years ago?" Kreevich asked. He sounded impatient.

Quist nodded. "I had to meet Craven and talk to him about that before I said yes or no. Jack Milburn brought him here."

"He's a really delightful man," Lydia said. She had dropped down on the bar stool next to Quist. "Cultivated, traveled all over the world, gentle, nice humor."

"But a man living with a wound that won't heal," Quist said.

Kreevich ground out his cigarette in the ash tray Quist had passed him and lit a fresh one. "How do I get you to tell me this story without a preamble?" He asked. "I'm investigating a double murder, you know."

Quist looked away down the room. "It was 1973," he said. "Most of the people in this country were listening to talk about Watergate. Bart Craven had retired from a job in the State Department because he was so in love with a ravishingly beautiful girl he had married about five years before that he wanted no other obligations in the world except to please her. She had been Maureen Tate, an English film actress, from all accounts a dazzling, vibrant, altogether charming girl. She was fifteen years younger than Bart—thirty in 1973, he forty-five. She was apparently as devoted to him as he was to her. Bart is wealthy. He could afford to give her anything in the world she wanted. She wanted, according to Jack Milburn and others, only to give him what *he* wanted. An ideal, apparently perfect marriage.

"In the spring of 1973 the State Department asked Bart if he would do the government a favor. There was some kind of touchy diplomatic maneuvering going on with some mid-Eastern ruler, oil in the picture. Bart had had successful dealings with this ruler before and the department thought he could be invaluable in this particular crisis, whatever it was. Bart agreed with some reluctance. He was reluctant because it meant leaving Maureen back here in New York for about a month. But he went, being a decent, patriotic man. How the mission worked out is not a part of the story. He was in constant

9

touch with Maureen by overseas telephone. Everything fine, everything just great. He was able to leave his freign base a couple of days sooner than he expected and he thought he'd suprise Maureen by just walking in the front door of their New York apartment. He did, but Maureen wsn't there when he arrived. No particular reason why she should have been. It was mid-morning. She could have been out shoping, lunching with friends. But, she didn't come home that afternoon, hadn't returned by dinner time."

"She never came home," Lydia said.

"No message? No word?" Kreevich asked.

"Not then, not ever," Quist said. "Friends had no idea where she was and might have gone. Bart fought panic for a couple of days. But when the day came that he'd been originally supposed to return passed and ther was no word from her he went to the police, Missing Persons. They found no trace of her. There was no indication that she'd packed to leave. Her jewelry, her clothes, her most intimate possessions were all intact in the apartment. She had apparently just walked out somewhere and that was that. No accident reported. No unidentifiedwoman's body anywhere."

"Bart has spent a fortune on private detectives over the past seven years," Lydia said. "He refuses to believe she's dead. He says he'd know it if she was."

"And he refuses to believe that she would leave him without a word, without a message. Leave him, perhaps, for reasons he can't imagine, but to leave him hanging, twisting—never," Quist said.

"But she did," Kreevich said.

"Gone, clean as a hound's tooth—as my father used to say," Quist said. "Bart's still keeping a private detective in clover, looking for her. Character named George Strock. You must know him."

"First-rate man," Kreevich said. "I'm surprised he'd go on taking money from Craven after all this time. He's not an operator."

"I talked to Strock," Quist said. "He told me he'd urged Bart to give up. He, Strock, hadn't come up with a single lead in something like six years. But he said Bart was so desperate, so anguished in his dependence on help from somewhere that he, Strock, didn't have the heart to close the door on him. 'She just went down a well somewhere and we don't have a clue to where to look for that well,' Strock told me."

"Craven felt his wife's disappearance so long ago might jeopardize his political chances?" Kreevich asked.

"He thought it might be a kind of variation on Chappaquiddick," Quist said. "I thought not. In any case, I liked him and agreed to handle his PR work if he decided to run."

"And tonight this Dr. Martine phones him to say he has some news of what happened to Maureen—Craven says."

"Let me tell you something, Mark," Quist said. "Bart Craven would go through the fires of hell if he thought the answer to Maureen's disappearance lay there. This doctor guy says he knows something and Bart would go to him, any time of day or night."

"And if this doctor and his nurse came up with something scandalous about Maureen, would he plug them between the eyes?" Kreevich asked.

"He just might," Quist said after a moment. "But you'll have to present me with a lot more than a guess to make me believe it."

Quist knew that his friend from Homicide was not a hunch player, but a thorough investigator who covered every possible angle on a case.

11

"He's not just looking for an easy out," Quist said to Lydia, who had complained that Kreevich was reaching. "He said at the start that Bart had 'opened a can of peas' by telling him the truth. But let's look at it from the point of view of someone who isn't Bart's friend, doesn't know him. A man in the public eye goes to visit a doctor after nine o'clock in the evening, a doctor who isn't his own medical man. Now let's pretend for a moment that Bart killed the doctor and his nurse."

"Why? I mean, what was his motive?"

"Just what Mark suggested. Dr. Martine brought up some scandal about Maureen. I think that's all Bart would need."

"Which means he went prepared to kill," Lydia said. "Which means he had a gun he managed to get rid of before the cops came."

"He would have had all the time he wanted," Quist said. "We don't know what time he really got to Martine's office. We only know what time he called the police, which he says was five minutes after he arrived and went looking for someone in the office. He could have arrived an hour before that, for all we know."

"So why does he tie himself to the case by saying Martine called him to say he had information about Maureen? That does open up a can of peas!"

"First, because it's the truth," Quist said. "Second, because he couldn't say he went there to have his blood pressure taken. Martine wasn't his doctor. There'd be no medical records on him in Martine's office. Too many people must know that he has a perfectly good doctor of his own somewhere."

"So he went there prepared to kill Martine," Lydia said. "Why didn't he just walk out after he'd done it? Why call the police and hang around for them to come, involving himself?"

"First, obviously, because he didn't do it," Quist said. "It happened just as he says it happened. But second, if he did do it, could he risk walking out? Who might have seen him come in and when? There are plenty of people around at eight or nine o'clock at night. He's a known personality. So he gets rid of the gun, calls the cops, and has an acceptable story for them when they come."

"With a friend like you a man doesn't need enemies." Lydia said, smiling at her man.

"I'm just showing you the kind of side-pocket shots Kreevich has to cover," Quist said.

"Shall I put on the omelette?" Lydia asked.

"I'm sorry, love, but I think I better get in touch with Bart." Quist reached for the phone on the corner of the bar and dialed a number. After about four rings a man answered, not Bart Craven.

"Is Mr. Craven there?" Quist asked.

"Who's calling, please?"

"Julian Quist."

"Julian! It's Jack Milburn here."

"I didn't recognize your voice."

"We've got hell to pay here, Julian."

"I know. I just had a visit from my friend Lieutenant Kreevich. Jack, you're going to have the press, the radio, and television people down on you as soon as the story breaks. I think, perhaps, I'd better come over. How is Bart?"

"In shock. He went to that quack's office to hear something about Maureen. He got there too late."

Some people make fortunes the hard way and are usually pretty tough customers after they get to the top. Others whose economic security does not come through their own work are likely to be on the soft side in crisis. Bartley J. Craven had inherited wealth from his father, steel the source, but he had not just leaned on his oars in fifty-two years of living. He had gone to Harvard, served his country in the Air Force in Korea, become a top figure in the field of international law, and been a valued member of the State Department. Money had never mattered to him because he had it, but he had never ducked the challenges that came his way. In the first forty years of his life he had been a loner. His mother and father had been killed in a railroad accident when Bart was twelve years old. There were no brothers or sisters, no intimate family of any sort. He was a poor little rich boy looked after by a young housekeeper, raised and guided by the impersonal trustees of his father's estate. He had met the challenge of growing up, of becoming a person in his own right, but he had done it in a lonely fashion. He had, literally, only one close friend, a boy he had met when he was first sent away to boarding school. Jack Milburn, a couple of years younger, was just the opposite of Bart. Jack was outgoing, surrounded by admiring friends, an athletic hero in school and college, almost spectacularly popular with girls and later women. Bart was shy, withdrawn, very private. But these two remained close over the years. Jack Milburn owed his friend for frequent financial aid from time to time, but that wasn't why he stuck to Bart. He liked him, respected him, admired him. Bart needed Jack's friendship because Jack was the one person with whom he could share his own dreams, fears, and hopes. There had never been anyone else until Maureen Tate came into his life.

She was a blind date arranged by Jack. Bart couldn't even remember now what the occasion had been; a party somewhere. He had been reluctant to go with a girl he didn't know, but he'd allowed himself to be persuaded.

14

He was forty, she was twenty-five, and she had knocked Bartley J. Craven flat on his keel. She was, he thought afterward, Jack's kind of girl—outgoing, popular, so damned vital. Why she had found it necessary to go on a blind date was never quite clear. The results were explosive on both sides. She wasn't the kind of girl he would ever had dared dream of for himself, and his shy, quiet, almost old-world respect and courtesy must have been something quite new to a dashing girl in the 1960s.

Three weeks after that first meeting they were married, and so marvelously, totally, wholly in love. They both blossomed; she from girl to gorgeous woman, he from a shy recluse to a full-blooded man.

"People enjoyed being with them," Jack Milburn told Quist when they first talked about Bart, "because they were—well, like you and Lydia, a perfect match. You like knowing, in this day and age, that there can be relationships like that."

And then the end, unexplained, brutal, disastrous. Maureen was just gone! No reason, no clue, nothing that Bart Craven could fall back on to make life bearable.

"And so when this creep called Bart last night"—it was now one o'clock in the morning—"he didn't stop to question, he just went," Jack Milburn told Quist. "It was like someone throwing him a life preserver at the last moment."

They were sitting in the book-lined library of Bart Craven's triplex apartment on the East Side. Quist had gone directly there after talking to Jack Milburn on the phone, but Bart had not yet put in an appearance.

"He called me when your police lieutenant had finished with him for the time being." Milburn said.

"It's going to bring up the whole thing of Maureen

again," Quist said. "That's not ideal if he's going to run for the Senate."

"Running for the Senate is just something to do, for Christ's sake!" Milburn said. "Oh, he's equipped for it. He'd be first class. But it's not bringing up the old story to the public again that matters. It's starting it up with him again. Did this Dr. Martine really know something? Is it possible there's at last a lead of some sort? To hell with what it does to his political chances. He's sent for Strock. That's what he's waiting for."

"The private eye?"

"Yes."

"To do what?"

"Who was Martine? What did he know? What *could* he have known?"

Quist was frowning. "Weren't there crackpots in the early days after Maureen vanished who thought they had clues? Weren't there attempts at extortion —squeeze a buck out of Bart because he was so eager for anything? Isn't that almost certainly what this Martine had in mind?"

"After seven years!" Milburn said. "Will they never let him alone?"

"I've got to be sure it wasn't a fake," Bart Craven said from the doorway.

Man of Distinction, Quist thought; dark brown hair, greying at the temples, elegantly tall in a custom-tailored Irish tweed suit, level brown eyes, good mouth and jaw. His handshake, as he reached Quist, was firm. You had to think this man was rock-solid.

"Thanks for coming, Julian."

"You're going to have an army of media people to handle any minute," Quist said. "I know most of them. I thought I could be useful, but I have to know exactly what your story is."

16

"Story? No story, just the way it happened," Craven said. "This man called. It was twenty-five minutes to nine. I was here alone. There was no need for my housekeeper, Mrs. Hoyt, to stay in. She'd gone to a film somewhere. I answered the phone."

"You have an unlisted number," Quist said.

"How did this Dr. Martine get it? I don't know. Perhaps he has a patient who's a friend of mine. The number isn't a big secret, Julian. I—I arranged for it way back then, when all kinds of crackpots, as you call them, were trying to collect a reward I'd posted for information that would lead me to Maureen. I just never went public again when things had quieted down."

"So this character who called you last night had it," Quist said. "How did it go with him, Bart?"

Craven moistened his lips. "I answered. He said, 'You don't know me, Mr. Craven. My name is Dr. Claude Martine. Are you still interested in information that might explain your wife's disappearance seven years ago?' I said my God, yes, I was. He told me his office was on East Thirty-eighth Street, ground floor of a remodeled brownstone. He gave me the number. 'If you'll come over here now, Mr. Craven, I can tell you what you've wanted to know for a long time.' I said I'd be there in half an hour, forty minutes. That was that."

"You didn't suspect it was a phony?" Quist asked.

"Goddamnit, Julian, when you've been as desperate as I have for so long you check out everything."

"So you got dressed, slipped your gun in your pocket, and took off," Quist said.

"What are you talking about, Julian? I don't own a gun."

"Sorry, Bart, I threw you a curve."

"I did have to get dressed," Craven said. "I was in

pajamas, dressing gown, in this room reading when the call came. I did stop to look in the phone book to see if there was a Dr. Martine at the address he'd given. There was."

"So you got dressed, took a taxi to East Thirty-eighth Street."

"Yes."

"Where did you pick up the taxi?"

"Right outside the building here. I was lucky. He was just cruising by."

"Go on, Bart."

"The taxi took me to Thirty-eighth Street. Private house, it looked like. Lights in the windows a couple of steps below street level—like most of those old brownstones. In the foyer there was just one name on the brass plate—Dr. Claude Martine. There was a main door leading into the house, and to the left there was a door marked 'Office—Walk in.' It was obviously after normal office hours so I rang the bell. Nothing happened. I tried the door and it was unlocked, so I went in. Well, he was expecting me, wasn't he?"

"Lights on in the office?"

"Yes. Desk for a receptionist, filing cabinets, all neat and orderly. Door to the right that I supposed led into a consulting room. I waited for someone to show, listened for voices. Nothing. So I went to the consulting room door, opened it and there were lights. I called out the doctor's name—and then I saw them!"

"Bodies?"

"Yes." Craven's voice was suddenly unsteady. "Man in a white office coat, woman in a nurse's uniform. Blood—my God—everywhere. I—I'm not a doctor, Julian, but I did serve in the Air Force in Korea, not quite thirty years ago. I've seen gunshot wounds, dead people. Nobody had to draw me a map."

18

"You examined them, touched them?"

"I didn't have to, Julian. They'd both been shot right between the eyes, foreheads blown away. You could have stuffed a beer can in the wounds."

"So?"

"So I did what anyone else would have done. I went to the outer office and called the police. I waited for them to come. Patrol car people arrived almost at once, looked things over, began taking a statement from me. The Homicide lieutenant was there before they were through."

"He lives just a couple of blocks away from Thirty-eighth Street," Quist said. "You didn't think you were in any kind of trouble, Bart?"

"What kind of trouble? I found a couple of dead people; I reported it. I waited for the cops. What trouble?"

"You told my friend Kreevich why you were there?"

"I had to explain why I was in the office of a doctor I didn't know. No reason not to tell the truth. I couldn't say I just walked in off the street to ask to use the bathroom!"

"What you did was to give him a possible killer on the scene with a possible motive," Quist said. "This doctor and his nurse told you something about Maureen and you shot them to keep them silent."

"You have to be joking!" Craven said.

"We told Kreevich he was reaching."

"We?"

"Lydia and I. But he'll have to take it from top to bottom. His job," Quist said.

"It's absurd," Jack Milburn said. He was sitting on the arm of a leather chair, looking jaunty in a navy-blue turtleneck sports shirt under a maroon jacket with bright brass buttons. "The whole thing has nothing to do with Bart. The doctor and his nurse were in trouble with somebody else; not connected to Bart or anything about Maureen—if there was anything about Maureen."

"Did Martine suggest you would be expected to pay for the information he had for you, Bart?" Quist asked.

"No. I've told you exactly what the conversation was."

"Money would have come into the picture when he talked to Bart at their meeting," Milburn said. "Somebody else he was hooking got to him first."

A little red light began to blink on the far wall.

"Front door," Milburn said. "That'll be Strock." He started out of the room.

"Or the news boys," Quist said. "If it's reporters, tell them Bart can't make any kind of statement till the police give him the green light. We don't want to talk to them yet."

Craven turned to Quist when they were alone. "You surely don't suspect I'm telling you anything but the truth, Julian."

Quist patted him on the shoulder. "I get paid for believing you, chum," he said. "And even if I didn't —get paid, I mean—I'd believe you. You're not so stupid as to have given them Maureen as a motive if you were guilty."

2

George Strock, the private eye Bart Craven had hired to find some trace of his Maureen, had a good reputation with the police. He didn't handle divorce or scandal cases. He specialized in missing persons, most often teenagers who had left home, leaving anxious and despairing parents behind. He worked compatibly with the Missing Persons Bureaus across the country. He helped them, they helped him. He had the kind of contacts that made him ideal to handle Bart's problem. Ideal or not, he'd come up with nothing in six long years; not a whisper, not even a good solid guess.

When Quist had agreed to work on Bart Craven's senatorial campaign, he had gone to see Strock at his apartment on West Tenth Street in the city. It was on the ground floor of another brownstone in a good, quiet neighborhood. It was about six months before the night Dr. Claude Martine and his nurse were murdered.

Quist had, for no reason, expected something out of the Chandler-Hammett school of private eye fiction. Instead he found a neat, quiet little man about sixty who might have been a country doctor or a college professor.

"I don't keep an office as such," Strock told him. "My work keeps me traveling all over these United States, looking for people. Mr. Craven asked me to see you. What can I do for you?" He was a round little man, good tropical worsted summer suit on that occasion, rather bright blue eyes that studied Quist through wire-rimmed glasses.

Quist laid it on the line to him. If there was anything sticky about Maureen Craven's disappearance, it was bound to surface during a political campaign, if there was to be a political campaign. Quist didn't want any surprises. He wanted to be prepared if there was something to be prepared for.

"I wish I could tell you there was something," Strock said. "I've been on this case for nearly six years. I haven't come up with a damn thing, Mr. Quist."

"Except a weekly check from Bart," Quist said.

"I've told him a dozen times he should forget about me. I was a bust, as far as his case was concerned. But hope keeps him looking, Mr. Quist. I'm all over the country—San Francisco, to New Orleans, to Chicago, to Palm Beach, to Boston; New York to Los Angeles. Up and down and back and forth, in every big city's Missing Persons Bureau. He insists, believes, that sooner or later, somewhere, something will show up. I'm not collecting a daily work fee from him; just a sort of retainer."

"And you keep looking?"

"It's become a kind of obsession with me," Strock said. "Let me show you something."

Strock took Quist out of the comfortable small living room into an adjoining room which could have been called an office. There was a flat-topped desk, filing cabinets, a telephone with an answering service attached. On the wall opposite the desk there were eight or ten photographs of a beautiful red-haired girl, in obviously studied poses.

"She was already a movie star in England when she met Craven and married him. Those pictures were taken about twelve years ago, when she was working. Five years of marriage, seven years missing. I got the pictures from Craven originally to take around with me. 'Ever see this woman?' You know the routine."

Maureen had certainly been sensational looking.

"Ever read a detective story called *Laura*?" Strock asked.

"Never read the book," Quist said, "but I've seen the old movie on the late show—Gene Tierney, Dana Andrews, Clifton Webb."

Strock nodded. "About a detective who fell in love with the portrait of a woman he thought had been murdered."

"But she turned out to be alive," Quist said.

"Would you believe I tried to convince myself it would be that way?" Strock said. "Craven kept telling me how wonderful she was, how bright, how gay, how witty, how tender—how altogether marvelous. Believe it or not, I began to dream about her. Like Laura, she would suddenly walk in the door, this door or the door in a hotel room in St. Paul, or Dallas, or Lexington, Kentucky. Of course she never did and she never will. I'm good at what I do, Mr. Quist. If there was one scrap of evidence, I'd have found it."

"Could there have been some other man in her life, someone from the days before she met Bart?"

Strock glanced almost lovingly at the pictures on the wall. "Can you imagine there weren't dozens of men after her? But no one who was remotely permanent before she came over here from England to make a film and met Craven. No one after she married him, God knows. They were glued together."

"Except for that last month when he was away."

"I must have memorized everything she did every day of that month. Lunching with friends, shopping, evenings at the theater, the ballet. Mutual friends. The day before Craven came home, early to surprise her, she left their apartment in the morning, told Mrs. Hoyt, the housekeeper, she was going shopping, would be back in the afternoon. That was it. Never seen again by anyone!"

"Mrs. Hoyt knew she hadn't come home that night?"

"Knew but wasn't distressed. She could have stayed with a friend, but none ever surfaced."

"You checked stores she might have gone to, places she may have had accounts?"

"In six years, Mr. Quist, I've checked every place in God's world there is to check. Shops, restaurants, neighborhood movies. She had friends, casual acquaintances, in the theater—she'd been an up-and-coming actress. Some of those people weren't a part of the regular circle of friends she and Craven saw in their marriage routine. But I saw them. Before I'd finished my first year on the case I went to England, at Craven's insistence. He had friends over there in the diplomatic corps. I had contacts at Scotland Yard. Theater people here put me on to film and theater people over there. A month's work added up to one, big, glaring zero."

"It's hard to believe she could just vanish."

"I haven't mentioned all the routine checks," Strock said. "Unidentified accident victims are on record somewhere; hospital records, morgue records. Pictures of Maureen have been circulated everywhere in this country, coast to coast, Canada to Mexico. Even if she were smashed up beyond recognition in some kind of catastrophe, there is no record of any unclaimed body that I haven't checked out."

"You must have come to some conclusions," Quist said.

Strock gave him a wry little smile. "Martians kidnapped her and she's somewhere in outer space," he said. "It's as complete a disappearance as that, Mr. Quist. But factually? Probably not complicated at all. Beautiful summer day, beautiful lady walking along a quiet side street somewhere. Some drug addict mugs her, drags her into a car, strips her of jewels. She probably had money in her purse."

"I thought no jewelry was missing."

"Only what she was wearing: a put-your-eye-out engagement ring, a gold wedding ring, a small diamond pendant. Those items never turned up anywhere, *not anywhere*! Her purse never turned up. She usually carried forty or fifty bucks in it. Credit cards; they never turned up. I said 'dragged her into a car' because she had to be taken somewhere, not left in an alley. The mugger slugged her, found he'd killed her, had to dispose of her. Maybe he dumped the body, weighted down, into the North River, the East River. Who knows, maybe into a garbage disposal shredder. All guesses, Mr. Quist. One thing I think I can tell you after all this time. No scandal, no other man, nothing that could damage Mr. Craven's campaign, the poor bastard. It's just a horror story without an answer."

That encounter with Strock had been six months ago. He came back on stage the night, or, rather, the early morning, after the double murder of Dr. Martine and his nurse. He walked into Craven's library looking like a man in mild shock himself.

"It just came over on the radio in my taxi," he said, after greeting Quist and Jack Milburn. "You found this doctor and his nurse, Mr. Craven?"

"Yes. He phoned me that he could tell me what had happened to Maureen," Craven said.

"You knew him? He's a friend?"

"Never heard of him before in my life," Craven said. "He must have known something, Strock."

"Known what?" Strock asked, his mild voice gone harsh. "That you're a rich man, willing to pay for any kind of information—after seven years?"

"He called me, out of the blue! He must have known something."

"How much did he ask for?"

"Nothing."

"You never got to talk to him?"

"They were dead, both of them, when I got there. But he must have known something, Strock."

"Oh, Jesus!" Strock said.

What a cruel thing, Quist thought. Violence, death, all mixed up with hope that had almost been abandoned. Bart Craven wasn't concerned about a double murder or any possible personal involvement in it. Had this unknown doctor really had information about Maureen? Was there something that could put an end to seven years of anguish? Even to have known for sure that she was dead would have been a relief.

"Forty-five minutes," Craven said. "Just forty-five minutes it took me from the time he called until I got there. If I'd been just a little quicker . . ."

"What is it you want me to do, Mr. Craven?" Strock asked.

"For God's sake, man, find out what he knew. There can be records in his office. Who were his friends, his patients? What part of the world did he circulate in that could have touched Maureen's past or—or present?"

"Stop it, Bart. She's not alive. You have to know that," Milburn said.

" 'Explain her disappearance' he said, not her death."

"The man was a cheap extortionist, playing on your grief," Milburn said.

"I've got to have that proved, Jack," Craven said. "If there's any chance at all . . ."

"Damn it, man, there isn't any chance!" Milburn said.

A middle-aged woman wearing a black dress, her face lined with sympathy, came into the room. Quist knew her to be Mrs. Hoyt, the housekeeper.

"I'm sorry to interrupt, Mr. Craven, but Miss Johns is on the telephone," Mrs. Hoyt said.

"Oh, thank you, Rachel. If it's on the radio, she's heard. I'll take it in my study."

Craven followed Mrs. Hoyt out of the room. Milburn brought his fist down hard on the arm of his chair. "If that bastard wasn't already dead, I'd kill him!" he said.

26

"You know anything about him, Mr. N asked.

"Never heard of him till tonight."

"The man had a house, an office, obvio tice," Quist said. "He had a nurse. I understa a receptionist somewhere. The man in charg case, Lieutenant Kreevich, knows you, Strock, well of you."

"Best homicide cop in New York," Strock said.

"He's obviously looking for the answers you want," Quist said. "Who was Claude Martine? I think Kreevich will be cooperative."

Strock glanced at the door through which Craven had gone. "Tell Bart I'm working at it, but try to convince him there is no reason on earth for him to have any hopes. I've worked on this case for six years. Maureen Craven has been dead since the day she walked out of this apartment seven years ago. There's not a shadow of a doubt about that."

"I've spent what seems like a lifetime trying to tell him that," Milburn said.

Lieutenant Kreevich is not overpopular with reporters for the media in the early stages of any case. Let them in the door too quickly and they are in your hair before you're ready to deal with them. The fact that a homicide has taken place is not, in police routines, a secret. Reporters covering the bureau know when a crime has been reported. They have working agreements with people from radio and television. The focal point on that night and early morning was Dr. Claude Martine's house on East Thirty-eighth Street.

Rusty Grimes, the big red-haired reporter for *Newsview* magazine, was one of the first of the media people to arrive on the scene. He was to run into a

27

dly enemy, Kreevich. Grimes had covered a dozen of the lieutenant's cases, and he knew that if he pushed too hard Kreevich would clam up on him and the rest of the army that would gather, demanding facts.

"Too early for me to tell you much, Rusty," Kreevich informed the reporter. "Someone who had an appointment with the doctor found him and his nurse shot to death, reported promptly to Homicide."

"Who was that someone?"

"I don't think so, Rusty—not till I've done with him."

"This 'someone' is a suspect?"

"Not yet, Rusty. You want to be useful and get a cherry on your ice cream later?"

"Of course."

"Who was Dr. Claude Martine? Who was his nurse, whose name appears to be Julia Prentiss? What is there to know about their personal lives? Who had an appointment with them before my 'someone' found them dead?"

"Robbery seems obvious, doesn't it?" Grimes said. "Doctor's office on the street level. A 'Walk in' sign. Creeps all over the city looking for drugs or anything else of value. Walk in, for God's sake, is an open invitation."

"I give you a start," Kreevich said. "There are all kinds of things of value in this place." They were standing in the reception room of the doctor's office. "Filing cabinets full of records, untouched. In the inner office where the two people were shot there are medicines, drugs, which my people tell me would have been worth a small fortune on the street, untouched. The doctor lived up above—three floors. A quick look shows valuable paintings, silverware in some quantity, expensive television sets, a hi-fi system, antique rugs, clothes,

28

some reasonably valuable jewelry in a room occupied by a woman—all untouched. Not robbery, Rusty."

"What then?"

"Someone wanted them dead, the doctor and his nurse. Why, of course, is the sixty-four-dollar question."

"Weapon?" Grimes asked.

"We think it was a small-caliber handgun. It went with the killer."

"Fingerprints?"

"The place is lousy with them, but we don't know yet who they belong to—the doctor, the receptionist whom we haven't been able to locate, the Prentiss woman, God knows who else."

"And your Mr. Someone's?"

"Perhaps, although he was careful when he found the bodies and phoned us."

"You're not going to be able to keep him a secret for very long, Mark."

"Oh, I'll tell you who he is if it's understood it's off the record until I give you the green light. And I mean off the record, just between us; nothing you pass on to your pals."

So much for having played straight with the lieutenant over the years.

"Who is he?"

"Bartley J. Craven," Kreevich said.

"*Bart* Craven?"

"The one and only."

"Oh, wow!" Grimes said.

A policeman came in through the street door. "We've found the other dame, Lieutenant," he said.

"The receptionist?" Kreevich asked.

"Yeah. Name of Ruth Taylor. She called in when she heard it on the radio."

"Bring her in," Kreevich said. He gave Rusty Grimes a tight smile. "Still off the record, but you can stay if you want."

Ruth Taylor was the prototype of thousands of office workers in the city—neatly dressed; a scrubbed, no-makeup look, which Kreevich guessed was very carefully applied; dark hair in a ponytail tied with a velvet ribbon; wide eyes behind heavy horn-rimmed glasses; a London Fog topcoat with a zipped-in lining; a scarf she'd removed from her head when she'd come in from the winter night, which she was twisting and turning between mittened fingers.

"This is Lieutenant Kreevich, in charge," the patrolman told her.

"I just couldn't *believe* it when I heard it on the radio," Ruth Taylor said. "They announced they were looking for the doctor's receptionist. I—I was just getting ready for bed, but I phoned in."

"We're grateful," Kreevich said.

Her eyes were moving quickly around the office, from the covered typewriter, to the ash tray on the desk, the closed engagement book, the pottery jar with pens and pencils in it, the box of paper clips.

"Everything about as you left it?" Kreevich said.

"Yes. Of course I haven't looked in the desk drawers or the files," the girl said.

"I'll ask you to do that later," Kreevich said. "When did you leave here?"

"About twenty minutes to six, I think," Ruth Taylor said. "The doctor's last appointment had gone in with him. The appointment was for five o'clock, but toward the end of the day he usually began to run late. The doctor never shortchanged anyone—for time, I mean."

"And who had that last appointment?"

"A Mrs. McAndrews, regular patient."

"You didn't stay till she left?"

"No need to. It's understood that after the last appointment goes in I can straighten up my desk and go home. The doctor or Miss Prentiss handled the phone after that."

"Let's have a look in the other office," Kreevich said.

"Oh, please Lieutenant! I can't bear to . . ."

"They're not there, Miss Taylor. The medical examiner's had them removed. I just want you to tell me whether things seem to be in place—or out of place."

She crossed the room behind Kreevich as if she was walking on thin ice. "I—I'm not as familiar with this room as the other," she said. "I mean, I don't get to handle things in here. But it *looks* normal, like Julia had prepared it for—for tomorrow." Her eyes widened. "There isn't going to be any tomorrow for her, or Dr. Martine, is there?" She pressed the back of a mittened hand against her mouth.

"Everybody comes to that day, sooner or later, Miss Taylor. The day when there isn't going to be any tomorrow. Let's go back in the other room, take your coat off, sit you down at your desk." He smiled at her. "Lots and lots of questions, Miss Taylor. First of all, the full name, address, and telephone number of your last patient. Mrs. McAndrews, you said?"

Ruth Taylor went to one of the filing cabinets. It was crowded with folders, case histories. "Mrs. Roger McAndrews," she said. "Her address and phone number . . .? Here we are." She gave them to Kreevich.

"She may have been the last person, except the murderer, to see them alive." Kreevich said. He handed the information to the patrolman. "Urge the lady, politely, to shuffle herself over here, Betts."

"Yes, sir."

Miss Taylor sat down at her desk. She had taken off

her topcoat and mittens. She kept flexing her fingers as if they were frozen, or stiff from arthritis.

"You read about this kind of thing every day." she said, "but you *know* nothing like it's ever going to happen to you. And then . . ."

"How long have you been Dr. Martine's receptionist, Miss Taylor?"

"Eight years last November," she said.

"Then you should be a gold mine of information. Tell me, has this always been his office?"

"He owns the building. He lives upstairs. I don't know for how long, but I gathered he'd been here for some time before I came to work for him."

"What was the doctor's speciality? No one is a general practitioner these days."

"The doctor is—was a dermatologist. Skin diseases and cosmetic surgery," the girl said. "Most of his patients are women, middle-aged. You take a little tuck here, a little tuck there. You know what I mean?"

"Face lifting?"

"Quite a lot. But you'd be surprised how much skin cancer there is. That's what most of the doctor's male patients have. Then there's birthmarks and blemishes. Gals don't want to have marks on them anywhere, you know?"

"I've heard," Kreevich said drily. "These files? They contain patients' records?"

"Each patient has a folder. What's kept here are current patients. There are stacks and stacks of folders on people who no longer come, stored in the basement. When a patient has an appointment I have her folder ready and on the doctor's desk in the inner office. I collect them and refile them when there's a break—like lunch, or when he's making a hospital call."

"Mrs. McAndrews's folder?"

"I noticed—it's still in there on his desk."

"Now we get down to the nitty-gritty, Miss Taylor," Kreevich said. "No one was scheduled to come in after Mrs. McAndrews?"

"I don't think so." Miss Taylor opened an appointment book on her desk. "No one. She was the last for yesterday."

"At half past eight last night Dr. Martine called a man, not a patient, and asked him to come over here to discuss something," Kreevich said. "That man got here at a quarter past nine and found the doctor and Miss Prentiss shot to death, so the murder happened in that forty-five-minute interval. The doctor was wearing his white office coat and Miss Prentiss her nurse's uniform. That suggests Mrs. McAndrews had a very long session —twenty minutes to six you say you left?—or there was a patient after her."

"I don't think Mrs. McAndrews could have been there all that time," Miss Taylor said. "She'd had a face lift some time back. She just came in to have him check on how it was doing. It shouldn't have taken more than fifteen or twenty minutes."

"The office uniforms suggest, then, that there was another patient later."

"Not in the book," Miss Taylor said. "Of course a patient could have called him after I left. The doctor could have arranged to see her—or him—and it wouldn't be in my book."

"But the nurse stayed late."

Miss Taylor looked down at her nervous fingers. "I guess it's no secret, Lieutenant. Julia Prentiss was living with the doctor. She'd have been upstairs with him."

Kreevich lit a cigarette and took a deep drag on it. "You've worked here eight years, Miss Taylor. You'd remember most of the patients?"

"I imagine I would. A look at the files and I'd remember."

"Was there a Maureen Craven? A Mrs. Bartley J. Craven?"

The girl's eyes widened behind her glasses. "I remember who she was. A big deal in the papers long ago, six or seven years. She disappeared, didn't she? But she certainly wasn't a patient in my time. I'd remember. There was so much talk about her."

"Was her husband a patient?"

"Bartley Craven? He's running for the Senate, isn't he?"

"It's in the wind."

"No. He wasn't a patient."

"You ever hear the doctor talk about the Cravens, Maureen in particular?"

"I don't think so. He may have, back when she disappeared. I mean, it was a big news story. But if he did, it wasn't because he knew her."

"Bart Craven is the man the doctor telephoned last night at eight-thirty and who found them both dead," Kreevich said. "You never heard him mention Craven?"

"Never. Oh, wow, no!"

The phone rang on Miss Taylor's desk. She looked at Kreevich.

"Go ahead and answer it," he said.

The girl picked up the phone. "Dr. Martine's office. Oh! Oh, yes, Mrs. McAndrews. Yes, the lieutenant's here."

Kreevich took the phone. The woman's voice was deep, throaty. "Lieutenant Kreevich?"

"Yes."

"I am Doris McAndrews, Lieutenant. There's a police officer here who says you want me to come to Dr.

Martine's office. I—I heard the awful news on television a little while ago."

"I have some questions I'd like to ask you." Kreevich said. "You appear to be the last patient the doctor saw."

"Lieutenant, I—I'm recovering from some cosmetic surgery the doctor performed. It's most embarrassing for me to appear in public. My face—my face is a mess. Can't I answer your questions on the telephone?"

"We can try, Mrs. McAndrews. You had an appointment with the doctor last night for—what time?"

"Five o'clock. But I didn't get in to see him till nearly five-thirty."

"Miss Taylor, the receptionist, says twenty minutes to six."

"I wasn't holding a watch on him, Lieutenant."

"What time did you leave?"

"A little after six. I was home at about six twenty-five. I remember because I tuned in the news on CBS radio. They give the time every four or five minutes. I walked home from the doctor's. It's only four or five blocks away. It was after dark. No one would—notice my face. It—it's going to be fine. The doctor said so, but it's going to take time."

"The nurse was with the doctor during your visit?"

"Miss Prentiss? Yes. My God, what a terrible thing to happen. Do they know who . . .?"

"Not yet, Mrs. McAndrews. Tell me, when you left was there anyone in the reception room?"

"I don't think so."

"I know Miss Taylor had gone home. But if you are shy about being seen, Mrs. McAndrews, surely you know whether there was someone there looking at you."

"There wasn't anyone."

"Well, thank you, Mrs. McAndrews. That, at least, is all for now."

Kreevich put down the phone. He looked at the girl and at Rusty Grimes, the reporter. "So there are a little more than two hours of Dr. Martine's life last night that need filling in."

"The last two hours of his life," Grimes said.

The complete story broke to the public in the early hours of the morning. There was no way Kreevich could cover the fact that Bart Craven had discovered and reported the murders of Dr. Martine and his nurse. It was on the police blotter before Kreevich was assigned to the case by Homicide. The only thing he'd been able to hold back for a while was what Craven was doing at the doctor's office. Craven himself, confronted by an army of press people, would certainly break it if Kreevich didn't.

Bart Craven wasn't primarily concerned with who had killed the doctor and his mistress-nurse. But what did the doctor have to tell him, and with the doctor dead, who else would know what that was?

There hadn't been a day of Bart Craven's life for the past seven years that hadn't started and ended with the same torturing questions. Where is she? What happened to her? Can no one come up with even a hint as to why she disappeared? When it appeared that answers were simply not going to be forthcoming, people close to him had tried to protect him, head him in some other direction, find something to occupy him, give him an interest in living.

"It's been a kind of lifework," Jack Milburn told Quist. The press had come and gone. Quist had handled them as best he could, but Craven hadn't helped to keep the story down. He had begged reporters to ask, publicly, for anyone to come forward who knew what Dr. Martine had been going to tell him about his vanished lady. By morning the whole story would be alive again, a sensation, Craven's wound open and raw.

"He isn't going to give a damn about running for the Senate now," Milburn said. "Without answers this time, he's just going to go down the drain."

"There's an answer somewhere," Quist said. "There has to be a way to find it." The first grey light of morning was appearing at the windows of Craven's library. Quist felt exhausted. He wanted to get back to Lydia, to reassure himself that she was there and in no danger. Spending hours with Craven's nightmare had made him create fantasies of his own.

"He's fixed on the idea that Martine had just stumbled on something, just now, just yesterday," Milburn said.

"Why would he have waited seven years if he knew something earlier, from the start?" Quist asked.

"God knows," Milburn said. He filled a glass with Scotch from a bottle that had appeared from somewhere in the course of a long night. He drank it down as though it were medicine.

"The girl who's with Bart now?" Quist asked.

She had come, early on; ash-blond, petite, probably in her thirties but almost childlike in appearance. Her name was Dilys Johns. She had been Craven's secretary for something like ten years, handling his appointments, his travel, his daily routine. She had started to work for him in the middle of his perfect marriage with Maureen, and he had never looked at her as a woman. There was only one woman in Bart's life. Dilys was just an important cog in his work machine. There was only one woman in Bart's life even after that woman was gone.

"Like hundreds of secretaries who work for important guys, Dilys is, of course, in love with him," Milburn said. "She's waiting and hoping, waiting and hoping, and, God help her, it's never going to happen. Bart's in love with a dead woman."

"When there's a doctor involved in a thing like this, you begin to have unpleasant thoughts," Quist said.

"Such as?"

"They had five years of marriage and no talk of children," Quist said. "Mind you, I know how that can be. Lydia and I have not wanted to bring children into this cockeyed world, which is why we live our lives in the style we do. But Bart and Maureen married."

"And wanted children," Milburn said. "Talked about it a lot in the beginning. Jokes about the kid, that he would probably have Bart's looks and Maureen's brains." He laughed. "That wouldn't have been a disaster, you understand. Bart's a good-looking man and Maureen is—was— an educated, cultivated, very bright woman."

"But they didn't have children," Quist persisted.

Milburn twisted in his chair. "Bart talked about it—oh, two, three years into the marriage. The one flaw in a perfect situation. They'd tried, and they'd tried to find out why they'd failed. Medical tests. I'm not sure whether Bart told me the truth. Some physical flaw in him. Maybe—in time . . ."

"Why wouldn't you believe him?"

"Because—well, because nothing on earth would have persuaded him to tell me, or anyone else, if the trouble lay with Maureen. She was perfect, she must appear perfect to everyone."

"Which brings us back to Dr. Martine," Quist said. "Strock has just told us he was a cosmetic surgeon, respected, on the up-and-up, Grade-A reputation.

Could Maureen have been a secret patient of his? Women are shy about nose jobs, or face lifts, or other artificial improvements to their looks."

"My God, Julian, she was just thirty years old when she disappeared, in full bloom, you might say. If she ever had any cosmetic surgery to remove scars, or blemishes, or other imperfections, it must have been before Bart met her, before she came to this country from England, before she was really launched on her film career. There are hundreds of publicity pictures of her from back in her early professional days. No scars, no nothing; most of all no change from the way she looked when she came into our lives here."

" 'Our lives'?"

Milburn nodded. "I was madly in love with her, as just about every other man who met her was. Only Bart had the magic for her. Strange, because I've known him ever since we were kids and he was never what we used to call a lady-killer. But he had everything for Maureen."

Quist got up from his chair and stretched. Bart and Dilys Johns were apparently not going to reappear. Bart was grimly answering phoned inquires from hundreds of friends, political backers, business associates, even from the White House, Quist learned later.

"I said doctors made you think of unpleasant things. Suppose Maureen didn't want a child. Suppose she had an abortion and something went wrong. Dr. Martine decided to collect . . .?"

"Dr. Martine was a cosmetic surgeon!"

"A doctor is a doctor is a doctor," Quist said. "Wrong operation for the wrong doctor."

"You must have sprung a screw, Julian," Milburn said. "A doctor butchers an abortion, patient dies. Doctor disposes of the body. Seven years later the doctor calls the victim's husband, having decided to tell all and send himself to prison for the rest of his life. You're not serious."

"I guess not," Quist said. He wanted to get out of here, back to Lydia and his own climate, where there was no pain, no shock, no horrors. He knew that his immediate future was going to be saturated with Bart Craven's agony.

3

As the day swung into life it turned out that *agony* was not the precise word to apply to Bart Craven's state of mind. It had been broad daylight when Quist got back to his apartment on Beekman Place and found Lydia dozing on the couch in the living room. She had waited up for him but she hadn't been able to stay awake. He felt a strange relief when he found her there, although there had been no real reason for him to be anxious about her. He knelt beside her and held her close while she came back into the world.

"You're all right?" she asked him.

"Now," he said. "It's crazy, but I began to be afraid you might disappear, too."

"What nonsense. The phone was endless until just a little while ago," she said. "People from our office wondering if there was any way they could be useful, a few reporters, including Rusty Grimes. And most insistent, and 'will you call him no matter what time you get back,' Paul Graves."

Paul Graves was the chairman of the committee preparing to handle Bart Craven's campaign for the Senate—if he decided to run. A lot of money had been raised, a lot of workers mobilized. Graves must be deeply concerned with what the night's violence might do to the future.

"Dilys Johns called just a few minutes ago."

"She's back there at Bart's apartment."

"I know. You'd apparently left just as she was trying to get to talk to you. Can she come over here now, at once?"

"Oh, God," he said. "I'm exhausted!"

"I told her she could," Lydia said. "I'm sorry, love, but she sounded so urgent. Can I make you coffee, eggs?"

"I suppose I'd better have something, including a shower and a change of clothes." He started for the stairway to the second floor.

"Carter beat Kennedy by two to one in Iowa," Lydia called after him. "Bush beat Reagan."

"Can you believe I couldn't care less?" he said, from halfway up the stairs.

Twenty minutes later he was back downstairs, shaved, showered, wearing a tweed jacket and slacks. Dilys Johns, Craven's tiny blond secretary, had arrived. She looked deathly tired. Lydia had provided her with coffee.

"I'm sorry to come after you, Mr. Quist. But it's better, I think, to try to talk to you here," she said. "You have no idea what he's like."

"Bart?"

She nodded. "Can you believe what's happened to him is hope?"

"I don't follow."

"He's convinced somebody knows what happened to Maureen. At last he's going to find out."

"Dr. Martine, who said he knew, is dead. The nurse who may have known is dead."

"Bart has convinced himself that the murderer knows and killed the doctor and the nurse to keep them quiet," Dilys said.

"There's probably no connection," Quist said. "The murders may not have any connection with Bart at all."

"I keep telling him they almost certainly don't," Dilys said. "He won't buy it. He thinks there's a killer around who knows what he wants so desperately to know."

"Is that possible, Julian?" Lydia asked.

"Anything is possible," Quist said. "But—just forty-five minutes between Martine's call to Bart and Bart's finding them dead. Was the killer there when Martine called? Did they have some sort of argument about whatever Martine meant to tell Bart? It doesn't make much sense. The chances are ten to one the killer, with some entirely different motive, arrived shortly after the call was made, killed his people, and walked out, not realizing that he was within minutes of being caught red-handed by Bart."

"The doctor and his nurse were dressed as if they were seeing a patient," Lydia said.

"According to George Strock, who's talked to the Homicide man, there's no record of any patient after six o'clock," Dilys Johns said.

"What is it you expect I can do, Dilys?" Quist asked.

"Talk to Bart," she said. "Persuade him that there's nothing to hope for, that this Dr. Martine had just thought of a cruel way to extract money from him. Persuade him to go on with his political campaign. He's got to have something to keep him occupied or he'll —he'll come apart."

"You and Jack Milburn are probably the closest people to him." Quist said.

"Which makes us useless!" she said. "He knows we love him, that we're only concerned about him, that we'd do anything to keep him from being hurt. You're something else. He trusts you as an outsider, a sophisticated, knowledgeable, worldly man. You know the political story inside out. Perhaps you can persuade him that he won't get a second chance. It makes no sense for him to throw away that chance. Persuade him to let the police and George Strock look for the killer."

"Who else?" Quist said.

"Bart has convinced himself that the killer knew what Dr. Martine knew about Maureen. He doesn't trust anyone, not Strock, not the police, not your Homicide man. They haven't come up with anything in seven long years. Bart has made up his mind to be his own detective, and nothing Jack Milburn, or Strock, or I can say will change his mind. If he got on the trail of something, Mr. Quist, he could be in terrible danger."

"It has occurred to me," Lydia said in a very quiet voice, "that it might be better if he never found the answer he wants."

"Meaning?" Quist said.

"Finding out what happened to Maureen might be harder to take than uncertainty," Lydia said.

"I'll talk to him," Quist said. "Trying to play Sherlock Holmes without any skills or resources is kid stuff."

Quist decided not to call Craven and tell him he was coming back. It wouldn't have made any difference if he'd decided to forewarn Bart. When he got to the apartment building off Gramercy Park he saw two police cars parked in front. Upstairs a policeman let him into Bart's apartment, where Lieutenant Kreevich was talking to Mrs. Hoyt, the housekeeper. Kreevich was not in the best of tempers.

"I should have locked your pal up," he said to Quist. "He's decided he's smarter than I am."

"That's against the law?" Quist asked.

"Wise guy!" Kreevich said. "Your Mr. Craven called me at headquarters a little after six while I was trying to write a report for the commissioner. He doesn't trust the police."

"So what's new?" Quist asked. "You haven't done anything for him for seven years."

"Nor has his own private eye, nor have his friends," Kreevich said. "So now he's going to take on the world himself! He's announcing it to the world, and out there, forewarned, may be a killer just waiting for him to get too close."

"So you've bought the idea that the murders of Dr. Martine and his nurse are connected with the disappearance of Maureen Craven?" Quist asked.

"I haven't bought a damn thing!" Kreevich said. He was seething. "Ten hours and we don't have a single blessed lead so far. No weapon, no witnesses, so far no explanation of the evening except Craven's—the phone call from Martine, the forty-odd minutes it took him to dress and get to Thirty-eighth Street where he found the bodies."

"Where is Bart now?" Quist asked.

"A lamb hunting for a killer wolf," Kreevich said.

"Where would he look?"

"Unless he knows something he hasn't told us, looking for an unknown killer in a city of eight million people," Kreevich said.

"It isn't unusual for him to wander off," Mrs. Hoyt said. "He's been looking for one person in a big city for a long time—seven years."

44

"He expected to find his wife out on the streets somewhere?" Kreevich asked.

Rachel Hoyt, Quist knew from some earlier conversation with Jack Milburn, was a great deal more to Bart Craven than an elderly domestic who made out his marketing lists and put away his laundry. She had been hired some forty years ago by an impersonal trustee to look out for a twelve-year-old boy in shock from the death of his parents. Bart Craven hadn't had very good luck with people he loved deeply. Rachel Hoyt, a childless girl of twenty, had taken over the intermittent care of Bart. It had been a daily business until he was finally sent away to boarding school. The trustee kept the Craven town house for Bart, and Rachel Hoyt was always there, on hand when he came home for a weekend or a vacation. For forty years now she had been maintaining his base home for him. She wasn't old enough to be his mother, but in the early stages of their relationship she had mothered him. Quist had wondered if, as Bart grew into manhood, Rachel Hoyt might have felt more than a motherly interest in this attractive guy who was, after all, only eight years her junior. Whatever, the tie between them was closer than man and servant. Maureen had evidently been delighted to have Rachel stay on when she and Bart married, and Rachel must have been a rock of strength for him when Maureen vanished. She was a dark, trim-waisted, efficient-looking modern woman, not some old nanny out of an English novel.

"I think there was a time when he did think he might run into her on the street," Rachel said, in answer to Kreevich's question. "In the beginning we all thought it was some kind of an accident, some kind of a violence. The police believed that, I think. But nobody ever found any leads, not the police, not George Strock.

45

Bart—Mr. Craven—was clutching at any possible explanation. One of his ideas was that something had brought on amnesia, loss of memory. He thought she might be wandering around, lost, without knowing why, in this neighborhood where she'd lived. He spent hours scouring the neighborhood, the neighborhoods where close friends had lived, the locations where there were restaurants or theaters they'd gone to. Maureen was mad for the theater; she'd been an actress, you know. He'd go, night after night, to watch theater audiences let out."

"And never anything," Quist said.

"Never anything," Rachel said. "He talked to me, just before he went out this morning, Lieutenant. I don't think he has any plan, any idea of how to go about finding this killer. It's an old obsession with him. If he wanders around out there, the answer he wants so desperately will drop in his lap. I've known him to be gone a day or two. He'll be back."

"You have any idea where he goes during those stretches, Mrs. Hoyt?" Kreevich asked.

"No. As long as I've known him, looked out for him, boy and man, he's always been a very private kind of person. I have known better than to pry. If I'd insisted on answers about that kind of thing, I'd have been long gone."

"Does he belong to any clubs?" Kreevich asked.

"The Harvard Club, The Players—which is just across the park here. I don't think he's been to The Players since—since Maureen went. He used to take her there. They're largely theater people, the members. Bart and Maureen invested in plays, you know. He qualified as a member as a Man of the Theater. Maureen loved the parties, the people she met there. He couldn't go back,

46

remembering her laughter, the gay times she enjoyed there."

"I've wondered why he's kept this apartment," Quist said. "Maureen must be everywhere. This is where they lived, where they loved."

"He couldn't give it up," Rachel said. She looked at Quist as if he wasn't quite bright. "Suppose she came out of her nightmare, wherever she is, came home and found strangers living here?"

"You sound as though you believe that might happen," Kreevich said.

Rachel let her breath out in a long sigh. "Of course I don't, Lieutenant. But that's what he wants me to believe, and so I don't debate it with him."

Kreevich reached for an ash tray and put out his cigarette. "I don't believe in miracles either, Mrs. Hoyt," he said. "But there is a cockeyed chance that a man looking for trouble may find it. If he should find the killer before we do, he could be dead before he could open his mouth to sound the alarm or deal with the situation himself. I want to know the instant he comes back. I want to make it clear to him what his position is. My job is to prevent violence as well as solve puzzles. I want you to call me when he comes back. It wouldn't be disloyal if you care for him. He's a sick man, Mrs. Hoyt."

"God help me, I'll call," Rachel said.

And so the day moved on, bright, sunny, cold.

It was only just after eight on that morning. Two friends, bundled up against the winds, stood alongside a police car outside Bart Craven's Gramercy Park apartment.

"Why are you riding herd on Bart?" Quist asked

47

Kreevich. "You really don't think he told you a straight story?"

Kreevich cupped a hand around his lighter flame as he lit a cigarette. "People with obsessions bother me," he said. "Seven years he's been looking for his woman. He doesn't look to the right or to the left without hoping to see her. Anything else he sees doesn't matter to him, doesn't register with him. So last night he gets a phone call. He's relaxed—in pajamas, dressing gown, reading. 'Come over to my house and I'll tell you what happened to your wife seven years ago,' a stranger tells him. After seven years! Does he stop to figure it's probably a fake? He does not."

"He stopped to see if Martine was in the phone book."

"To make sure he had the right address, he was that charged up. He doesn't think about what he may be walking into. He dresses, hails a cab out here. Can he describe the cab driver or give us his license number? Of course he can't. He gets out in front of Martine's house. Did he see anyone coming or going? He doesn't remember. He wouldn't have noticed a small army unless his missing lady was one of the soldiers. Anyone in the vestibule of the building? He doesn't remember. This is a man operating in a fog, Julian; a panic, a hopeless dream keeps him running in all directions at once. If I could get him to hold still for a minute, try to remember anything that could help us, we might begin to move."

"I should think Dr. Martine would be your prime interest—and his girl-friend nurse."

"I'm on the way to St. Margaret's Hospital now to talk to people there," Kreevich said. "According to his receptionist, Martine was on the staff there. We'll see what we see."

"You keep more than two balls in the air you come up

with more than one answer," Quist said. "I'll be interested to know what you come up with on Dr. Martine. St. Margaret's is a first-rate institution; you'd be inclined to believe a doctor on the staff there would also be first-class."

"First-class doctor doesn't mean he was a first-class human being," Kreevich said.

"I've been having an itch for the last hour or two, Mark," Quist said. "Bart Craven says he didn't know Dr. Martine, never heard of him until he called tonight. So the voice on the phone wouldn't have been recognizable. Just a man's voice. It didn't have to be Dr. Martine, Mark. Dr. Martine and his nurse could have been dead on the floor of that office when that call was made."

"By the killer?"

Quist nodded.

"To get Bart Craven on the scene and implicate him?"

"Could be," Quist said. "All anybody had to do to get Bart to the scene of a crime was to hint—just hint —there might be some news about Maureen."

"So that would have to be someone who knew how he would react to such a suggestion. A friend?" Kreevich made an impatient gesture. "Theorizing grows long grey beards. You want to be helpful, Julian?"

"Of course."

"With people being mugged and banks being robbed on every two blocks in this city, I can't have an army of cops out looking for Craven. But his secretary, the Johns girl, and Mrs. Hoyt know who his friends are; you're in contact with—what's it called? The Committee to Elect Bart Craven to the United States Senate? A small army of people who know him by sight and care about his future. Can you mobilize them to go out into the streets and find him?"

"Quite a number of them, I should think."

"So go, friend. If they find him, tell them to sit on him until I have a chance to talk to him."

It was just short of twelve hours since someone who said he was Dr. Martine had called Bart Craven on the telephone and plunged him into the center of a violence. The investigation was moving at a snail's pace. The killer, Quist thought, could be out of the country by now.

Dr. Ira Powell, executive director of St. Margaret's, looked more like a business executive than a physician. Hospital politics, fund raising, negotiations with sponsors and staff, with matters of health left to others, Kreevich thought. Powell had curly grey hair, crew cut, shrewd pale eyes used to assessing people, and a nervous habit of drumming with well-manicured fingers on the edge of his wide desk. Scandal involving anyone on his staff, administrative or medical, was a disaster to him. Substantial donors to St. Margaret's operating funds could become disenchanted.

"When I heard the news I was shocked beyond words, Lieutenant," he said, in a crisp, businesslike voice. If he meant to sound as if he was grieved for a colleague he didn't make it with Kreevich.

"I take it you knew Dr. Martine personally," Kreevich said.

"Of course I knew Claude. He interned here, later became a resident on our surgical staff. Finally went into private practice, but St. Margaret's remained his hospital affiliation." There was a folder on Powell's desk and he edged it toward the Homicide man. "I had this ready for you. It's his record here, his history as a staff doctor."

Kreevich flipped open the folder. On top of the stack

50

of documents was a photograph of a dark-haired, handsome man.

"He was good looking," Kreevich said.

"Well, surely you knew that, Lieutenant. I mean, you saw him . . ." The words drifted off.

"His face was pretty well mutilated by the gunshot that killed him," Kreevich said.

"Good God!"

"The nurse, did you know her? Miss Prentiss?"

"Julia Prentiss was on the staff here. That's where Claude met her, I think. When he went into private practice, she left to go with him."

"You knew they were living together?"

"His private life, after he was no longer a resident here, was none of my business," Powell said.

"You have a picture of her?"

"I can get her folder for you," Powell said. "It's in what we call 'the archives.' She hasn't been connected with us for a number of years, about seven or eight, I think." He pressed a button on his desk and an attractive secretary popped in the door almost instantly. She could have been listening, Kreevich thought. "Miss Lewis, would you get Julia Prentiss's folder from the archives, please."

"At once, Doctor."

Kreevich glanced at the information in the folder. "Cornell, Johns Hopkins, interned here. How did you rate him as a doctor?"

"The very best—at his specialty," Powell said.

"Cosmetic surgery?"

"My dear Lieutenant, we don't do that kind of thing here at St. Margaret's. That's not a health hazard or an emergency of any sort. Claude went into that when he became his own man. We have one of the best burn units

51

in the country. People caught in fires, plane wrecks, car accidents involving burns are brought here from all over. Claude started in that unit early on. Skin grafts, that kind of thing. He's still our top man when we are faced with a serious emergency involving burns. His skills, I suppose, led him into the cosmetic field when he went private. Lots of money in it."

"He owned a house that must have cost plenty."

"Let me tell you, Lieutenant, the prices aging ladies will pay to have their faces refurbished would stun you."

"Was he a young man of means when he first came here as an intern?"

"Lord, no. If you look at the records carefully, you'll see he practically worked his way through medical school—car wash, short-order chef, God knows what else."

"And he didn't get rich here, working as an intern or a resident?"

"Not in the cards, Lieutenant."

"But he left here and set up a rather rich-looking practice—a house in the Murray Hill area, valuable paintings, all the outward evidences of a wealthy man."

Powell hesitated. "About ten years ago there was an airline disaster in the midwest—somewhere in Ohio. We had eight or ten burn victims here. One of the victims was the teen-age daughter of a very rich Texas oil man. Claude did something like a miracle on that girl, repairs to bone damage, skin grafts."

"They can do that after burns?" Kreevich asked.

"Not always," Powell said. "Sometimes the damage to the bone structure is too great to restore anything like original appearance, skin grafts won't take. But in the case of this Texas girl you'd have to see progress pictures to believe it. The father—I never heard him called anything but Tex Delaney—was almost pathetically grateful. I know he offered to help Claude set himself up in private practice. How much was involved I don't know. It isn't, of course, any part of our records."

"Do you know where this Tex Delaney lives?"

"An address, no." Powell laughed. "Texas. But I guess it wouldn't be any harder to find out where Tex Delaney lives in Texas than it would to find out where a Rockefeller lives in New York."

The secretary returned with the records on Julia Prentiss. Kreevich took both files for someone to study. "Would it occur to you, Doctor, that Claude Martine was so in love with his expensive way of life that he might be willing to blackmail someone to keep the funds coming in?" he asked.

Powell tilted his head back and his laughter seemed quite genuine. "He wouldn't have to, Lieutenant. All he had to do was name his price for an operation and he got it. A lady wants to look younger, she'll give a gold mine if she has to."

"At today's gold prices?" Kreevich asked drily.

"If that's what Claude demanded. He—he was the best."

Kreevich stood up, tucking the folders under his arm. "You've heard the story on TV or radio, I take it."

"You mean how Bartley Craven found them?"

"Yes. You know about the disappearance of Bart Craven's wife some years ago?"

"It was a big news story at the time."

"It's not yet in today's news, Dr. Powell, but Craven says he got a phone call from Dr. Martine, a man he didn't know, about forty-five minutes before he found Martine and his nurse dead. He says Martine told him he knew what had happened to his, Craven's, wife seven years ago."

"My God!"

"Is there any way you could know whether Mrs. Craven was ever a patient of Dr. Martine's?"

"Certainly not here at the hospital," Powell said. "It should be in his own records if she was a private patient. Seven years ago Claude Martine had gone on his own."

"It isn't," Kreevich said.

"I'm trying to remember, Lieutenant. Wasn't Mrs. Craven quite a young woman when she disappeared?"

"About thirty."

Powell shook his head. "Women don't get face lifts at thirty, Lieutenant. Forty-five, fifty—that's about the time. What Claude could have known about Mrs. Craven. I can't begin to guess, but it surely wasn't a face lift."

At least three of them cared deeply for Bart Craven in very personal ways. Jack Milburn had been his one close friend since boyhood. Rachel Hoyt had cared for him and his needs on a day-to-day basis for almost forty years. Who knows, she could have had other emotions for him as they both matured. Dilys Johns had shut herself away for years from any other kind of relationship to handle his career needs. Quist wondered if, in these last seven tragic years for Bart, Dilys had offered love and intimacy, willing to be, forever, second best to a dead woman. These three, Quist was certain, would go the limit for Bart, whatever that called for.

Quist wasn't so sure of the other three. To Paul Graves, Quist thought, Bart was just a horse to bet on in a big race. He was chairman of the committee to elect Bart to the Senate. As long as the odds favored Bart, all of Paul Graves's personal charm, which was considerable, his political contacts, which were wide, his expertise in this kind of gamble, which he'd used with great success many times before, were at Bart's disposal. Let the odds shift, Quist thought, and Paul Graves would be off to the mutual windows to bet on another entry. Graves was tall, dark, wore expensive clothes, his hair styled, not barbered. He had a perpetual, dazzling smile that said to both friends and complete strangers, "I care for you!" Yet the minute the odds changed all you would be likely to see of him would be the back of his broad shoulders. Graves only bet on winners, Quist thought. Could he be counted on now? That might depend on how good a salesman Quist was.

The other two people gathered in Quist's very chic office, with its chrome-trimmed furniture and its abstract modern paintings, were strictly from the world of politics. Tom Molloy, a giant, cigar-smoking Irishman, with a fringe of red hair around a shiny bald head, was the party's man in the city. He had spent his life trading votes for patronage. Senator Ralph Metzger was a man on the fence. At seventy-four, he was the perfect picture of an old world statesman—a mane of white hair, bushy dark eyebrows, bright blue eyes. The senator could do his arithmetic. If he ran for a fourth term in the Senate he would be eighty years old when his term expired. He'd had enough, but he was a party man. If the party didn't come up with someone they could elect, Metzger would, reluctantly, run again. He would be a shoo-in. The party had decided Bart Craven was their best bet to replace the senator. Now Molloy and Graves and the other party leaders would have to decide whether Bart Craven's involvement in a brutal murder took him out of the running.

"You have to understand, Mr. Quist," Tom Molloy, the big Irishman, said, "it has nothing to do with what we personally think of Bart. You'd have to have ice water in your veins not to feel sympathy for the man. We in this room know what a decent man he is, what a competent man he is. But to the people who will go to

55

the polls to vote he's just a name, just a face they see on their TV screens and in their newspapers, and if there's scandal or mystery attached to him, people will think the worst."

"Didn't you ever do your duty as a citizen, Tom," Quist asked, "or is that too dangerous for a professional politician?"

Molloy grinned. "I'm ready for the punch line," he said.

"No punch line, Tom," Quist said. "But I'm supposed to be your expert on what people will or won't buy. A man walks into his doctor's office, finds the doctor and his nurse shot to death. Being a good citizen, he calls the cops and waits for them to come. That means he's a man you couldn't trust to represent you in the United States Senate?"

Paul Graves patted his expertly styled hair to make sure it was properly in place. "Only two things wrong with that, Julian. The doctor wasn't *his* doctor. He wasn't there to get a flu shot! He had to tell the whole cockeyed world that he was there because this doctor, whom he didn't know, was going to tell him what happened when his wife disappeared seven years ago. So that carefully interred mystery, we thought, is opened up again. Who knows what, Julian? It's going to hang over our heads like a ticking time bomb. Is there some kind of old scandal that will come to light after we're committed to Bart? We can't turn back, you know, after we've given him the green light."

Quist smiled at Senator Metzger. "The senator can always pick up the ball for you if Bart fumbles."

The senator shook his white head. "If the boys tell me now that they need me to run, that's one thing. But once I've said no, Mr. Quist, that will be that. I will have pulled the plug on the bath water."

"So can we afford to let him pull the plug?" Tom Molloy asked in his hearty voice.

"That isn't really the question, is it, Tom? Is there any question you can't get Bart Craven elected if you decide to run him? That's the question, isn't it?"

"Where is he?" Paul Graves asked, his voice sharp. "He has to know that, after last night, there are decisions to be made, evaluated. He just walks out!"

"The man had a shocking experience, only last night," Quist said. "A double shock. He thought he was going to hear something about his wife's disappearance, and he walks in on two people brutally murdered. He should be here, full of jokes?"

"I think you gentlemen should know," Rachel Hoyt said, "that this isn't unusual behavior for Bart—Mr. Craven. Since Mrs. Craven vanished seven years ago he has developed a habit of taking off for a few hours, even a couple days. When what he's thinking about, or facing, is too painful, he needs to be alone, think it through, get pulled together on his own."

"Mrs. Hoyt has taken care of Bart since he was twelve years old," Quist said. "She knows him better than any of us."

"I know him pretty well, too," Dilys Johns said. "I've been his secretary for ten years. I think you have to understand, gentlemen, that yesterday at this time Bart Craven was quite prepared to run for office, to embark on the rigors of a political campaign." The tiny blond woman's voice was unsteady. "I think for the first time in seven years he had spent a month or six weeks in which he'd finally persuaded himself that Maureen was gone, that there was never going to be an explanation or an answer. He talked to me about it. He was resigned. He was prepared to start living a normal, active life again. And then this monstrous doctor, a man Bart

57

had never heard of, called him on the phone and—and . . ."

"Clawed open an old wound," Quist said.

"What is this crazy talk that he's going to find the killer, that the killer knows the answer? That doesn't sound like a man who's ready to live a normal life," Paul Graves said.

"He was bleeding," Quist said.

"Oh, screw that kind of talk!" Graves said. "The Homicide people want us to have all the party workers out on the streets looking for him. What do we tell them? What kind of 'normal' is that?"

"A man doesn't have to make sense in the first hours of being in shock!" Quist said.

"He'll come back, normal as you please," Rachel Hoyt said. "Just give him a little time to work it out for himself. He's lived with a tragedy, gotten over it, and then had it dumped in his lap all over again. He needs time. I don't think you have to look for him. I think you should let him alone. When he comes back he'll say yes or no about running for the Senate. If he says yes, you can count on him all the way. If he says no, you can count on that, too."

"Look," Quist said, businesslike, "my job—if I still have one—is to sell Bart Craven to the voters of this state. So, tell them the truth. You think you may make the voters doubt him. I think I can make them sympathize with him."

"His record, his experience is first rate," Senator Metzger said.

"Suppose his wife ran off with some Hollywood glamor boy?" Graves asked.

"And stayed hidden for seven years? Come on, Paul," Quist said. "This is a modern world. Marriages break up, but the people don't go into hiding! Maureen

58

Craven was the victim of some kind of a senseless violence; a mugger, a sex nut. She was killed and disposed of. There's no scandal, unless you choose to call the violent world we're living in a scandal."

"Tell me, Mrs. Hoyt," Tom Molloy said, his cigar moving from one corner of his mouth to the other, "you say that going off by himself has not been an uncommon thing. You say he should be back in a few hours, a day, maybe two days."

"That's the way it's always been, Mr. Molloy," Rachel said.

Molloy looked at the two other men. "I say let Mr. Quist handle the press. Let him go ahead with selling sympathy. Bart will come back in forty-eight hours and he'll say yes or no to us. We have that much time."

"Not much more," Graves said. "I don't like it."

"I'll bet you money will start to pour in for his campaign when people hear what a lousy thing has happened to him," Quist said.

"And we have our workers look for him, the way this Lieutenant Kreevich wants us to?" Graves asked.

"Look for him, and if they find him say hello and let one of us who's close to him know where he is."

"He'll come back—today, tomorrow," Rachel insisted.

Senator Metzger stood up from his chair. "I go along with Tom," he said. "Let's play the cards as they fall for a couple of days. I know Paul thinks every hour is important, but I tell you, friends, I've been dreaming of next summer's fishing. Give me a couple of days, even if you won't give them to Bart."

4

A lot of people walked the streets of the city that day, keeping an eye out for Bart Craven. Nobody saw him. He had not visited his clubs. Someplace in the city there must be a hideout Bart had used over the years when these moments of being alone were necessary to him, but no one close to him had the faintest idea where it might be. When Bart wanted to be secretive, he was evidently a master at it.

Quist had handled Rusty Grimes and the rest of the press corps with his usual skill. There was no hiding Bart's involvement in the Martine murders, nor his grim reason for being there. There was no way to stop the reporters from reopening the whole mystery of Maureen's long-ago disappearance. But Quist made it clear that Bart was a man who had suffered enough, who needed and was entitled to some consideration. The late afternoon radio and television shows indicated that the media meant to keep Bart in the background for the time being. He was probably going to run for the Senate. He had a distinguished career in the State Department. Dr. Martine, who had promised information he was never able to deliver, was featured. The rich Murray Hill doctor, sculptor of hundreds of beautiful and famous faces, head man of St. Margaret's highly efficient burn unit, had probably been the victim, in his walk-in office, of drug addicts. Someone mentioned that the doctor and his nurse, Julia Prentiss, were POSSLQs —a term used by the census takers to identify people of the opposite sex sharing living quarters. That would be enough to satisfy the sensation seekers for a while. Maureen, for the present, was to be left in peace.

"But not for long," Kreevich said. It was about six in the evening and he was sitting at the chrome-trimmed bar in Quist's apartment. "The longer your friend stays hidden, the sooner your soft soap will wear off, Julian, and the whole Craven story will become the lead item."

"POSSLQ!" Quist said. "We live in a world of letters and numbers. Do you know I'm 104-33-2501 at Social Security? At my bank I'm 0222-0116. When I'm driving my car I'm 08650978. POSSLQ!"

"They probably didn't enjoy their life style any less, in spite of the Census Bureau," Kreevich said. "Interesting man, the doctor. Care to hear about him?" He was enjoying a vodka martini on the rocks.

"As long as you promise to speak ill of the dead," Quist said.

"A woman chaser as an intern," Kreevich said. "Most of the young nurses at St. Margaret's had at it with him at one time or another. Some of them still looked a little misty-eyed when I asked about him. Then came the big plane crash and the rich Texans, the Delaneys. Gloria Delaney, the teen-aged daughter, was in pretty horrible shape when she was brought to the burn unit at St. Margaret's. Martine, from all accounts, turned burned hamburger into a beautiful face again. Bones restructured, skin grafts."

"That's possible?" Quist asked.

Kreevich shrugged. "Fifty-fifty chance, according to the head man at St. Margaret's. Sometimes the results are sensational, sometimes the unhappy victim spends his life looking like something out of a monster movie. In this case the girl might have looked a little patchworky stark naked, according to Dr. Powell. Skin was taken from so many places to make what was normally visible handsome again. Tex Delaney, oil and cattle and God knows what else, loved his daughter beyond Powell's ability to describe. He gave the hospital a million bucks, and he set Claude Martine up in private practice. I talked to him on the phone, long distance. He reacted, when he heard what had happened to Martine, like he'd lost a son. He bought that house on Murray Hill and gave it to Martine, and contributed handsomely until the doctor got his practice going. Then, believe it or not, Martine began paying him back. He paid for the house, he paid back all the money the old man had advanced him for several years. He needn't have, Delaney told me. It was meant as a gift, out of eternal gratitude. So Dr. Martine seems to have had some scruples."

"The house, the property, is probably worth twice what he paid for it."

"Maybe four times," Kreevich said.

"Who inherits it?" Quist asked.

"Would you believe Julia Prentiss?"

"Who inherits from her?"

"Would you believe we haven't been able to find a will? Martine's laywer, a man named Wilshire, says he tried to get the Prentiss girl to draw up a will, but she 'just never got around to it.' But there are other highlights."

"Oh?"

"Martine gave a patient a new face, and in the process a baby. She sued and won support of the child in a paternity action. He's been paying for some years. That baby's going to grow up in luxury if the figures Wilshire gave me are correct. An angry husband—another woman's husband—put Martine out of action for about

62

three months; beat the hell out of him in the men's room at the hospital a couple of years ago. He just couldn't leave women alone, it seems."

"But the Prentiss girl stayed with him."

"Maybe she didn't mind," Kreevich said. "Maybe she had something on him. Whatever, she had jewelry, furs, clothes. She was doing fine. They lived in pretty elegant style upstairs in that house."

"And he was going to blackmail Bart, to maintain that life style?"

"We don't know that," Kreevich said.

"You got another explanation?"

"I'm not in love with your Mr. Craven," Kreevich said. "We have his story, but we don't have, and probably never will have, Martine's story. We don't know, except that Craven says so, that Martine really called him with the word that he knew about Maureen. No such thing may have happened. We don't know, yet, if there may have been some other relationship between Martine and Craven. Craven says he never heard of Martine until that phone call last night—if there was a phone call. What I'm looking for, Julian, is something that will tie those two together, something that has nothing whatever to do with the missing Maureen."

"Not something that will separate them, definitely, in your mind?"

"Anything definite, on either side of the coin," Kreevich said. He sounded tired, a little discouraged. "Your man doesn't act sensibly, Julian. He's a candidate for high political office. He runs into a sticky situation, and instead of holding still so his friends can rally around him, he ducks out. It's not normal."

"He has been doing just that for the last seven years when the tension was too much for him," Quist said.

"How many men do you know whose cherished wives vanished without a trace? If you do know some, maybe you know what's normal behavior for them."

"I suppose it's an occupational disease," Kreevich said. "I don't believe anyone's story till it proves out. Your guy's story of what happened last night is never going to prove out. No way to prove there ever was a phone call, or if there was one, what time it was made. The housekeeper was out at the movies. She can't verify a call. No one left alive at Martine's who can verify it. So we don't know, except for Craven's say-so, what time he really went to Martine's. He could have been there a long time before he says he was, killed a couple of people, taken time to dispose of any clues—and his gun. *Then* called us!"

"The taxi he says he took there?" Quist asked.

"We're checking. Maybe he took one, maybe he didn't. It wasn't too far to walk, not for a man who's spent seven years walking and walking around town. Some taxi drivers don't enter a short trip on their record. It's a way to chisel a few bucks out of the cab company. Not enough gas used to have to account for it on the trip sheet. If that's the way it was, the driver won't come forward."

"Let a man be charged with murder for three or four bucks?"

"Could be."

Lydia, who was tending bar, handed the detective a fresh martini. "Doesn't the man's history count for anything, Mark?" she asked. "Good school record, college record, war record. Trusted with important secret negotiations by the State Department. A career of public trust, you might say. Why don't you lean toward believing a man with that background?"

64

"Whatever drives a man to murder," Kreevich said, "drives him away from familiar patterns, away from truth. As long as a person is a suspect I don't believe anything he or she tells me until it proves out. Your Mr. Craven hasn't been his normal, substantial self for *seven years*! You two never knew him when he was his normal, substantial self. You apply what you know about his past, his education, his service record, his diplomatic career to the man you know. But the man you know has been off his rocker for *seven years*! No job, no career, wandering around the city looking for a dead woman, keeping a private detective on his payroll for all that time, periodic disappearances—like a drunk or a drug addict. That isn't the man whose history you say is so great, Lydia. Sick, thrown off balance by tragedy, someone for whom you may feel sympathy and compassion, but incapable of a violence if someone presses the right button? It's got to prove out for me, friends."

Kreevich wasn't being totally unreasonable, Quist told himself. "So I want it to prove out, too," he said. "And the sooner the better, Mark. I've got a very well-paying job selling him to the voters of New York State. I can sell him, I think, if you don't keep throwing curves at him in public. Every instinct I have tells me you're wrong."

"Let him stop hiding and talk," Kreevich said. "A real good hitter can handle a curve ball. That's why he's in the big leagues."

One thing he could be grateful for, Quist knew when Kreevich left, was that the detective wouldn't spring surprises on him. He'd be kept posted by his friend. The other side of that coin was that, if anything came Quist's way that worked against Bart Craven, he'd have to play the same honest way with Kreevich.

"He has you doubting?" Lydia asked.

"He's right, you know. We never knew Bart before his trouble. When Jack Milburn introduced me to him, asked me to handle his campaign, I had every reason to believe he was over the hill, out of the woods. Something threw him back into his own private hell again last night. I tend to believe it was just what he says it was, a phone call from someone he didn't know that promised him information he had to have if it existed. He would do just what he said he did, go to Dr. Martine to get it. When he was too late, the old horrors took over again. Somewhere there was an answer, and he'd missed it. He'll come out of his hiding place, wherever it is. Whether he'll go ahead with a political career is something else again. He may decide that, without an answer, there is no way to forget the past. I think I might decide just that if I was in his shoes. Don't ever walk out on me, love, without telling me why."

"A promise," Lydia said.

The evening wore on, not peacefully. The phone was almost constant. People kept calling with the same question. Jack Milburn, Dilys Johns, Rachel Hoyt, Rusty Grimes, the *Newsview* reporter. Had Quist heard anything from Bart Craven? None of them had. All of them were checking with each other. A desperate man they cared for, or had a vital interest in, was somewhere, needing help. The political people had had their party workers on the lookout, but there had been no sign of Bart. No one had the remotest idea where to look.

Quist spent some time working on press releases dealing with the projected campaign. Lydia handled the phone calls which began to peter out as the evening passed. Tomorrow would be busy, and vital. If Bart wasn't available to the press corps, there would have to be explanations. A last look at the television news indicated that the police had offered nothing new on "the Murray Hill killings," Quist and Lydia finally turned in.

It was daylight when Quist came out of a deep sleep, aware that the little red telephone light was blinking on the bedside table. There was no bell on the phone, but the red light, flashing on and off, could always bring Quist back from however far off he was in sleep. He glanced at Lydia, happily comatose beside him, and picked up the phone.

"He's struck again," Kreevich said. His voice was flat, impersonal, as though he were talking to a stranger.

"Who struck what?" Quist asked, still a little foggy.

"Another murder in the house on Thirty-eighth Street," Kreevich said. "Have you heard anything from Craven?"

"No. What's the score, Mark?"

"We left Martine's house locked, sealed up," Kreevich said. "Patrol car passing by every ten-fifteen minutes. There's a man named Pete Gamage who is the superintendent-caretaker for three or four houses on the block. He took care of Martine's house. He went to bed around ten o'clock. He could see Martine's house from his own apartment—dark, no lights. Around three o'clock he woke up; had to go to the bathroom. He noticed there was a light burning on the second floor of Martine's house. He woke his wife, told her he was going over to see what was cooking. She tried to persuade him it was the police, but they'd told him they were through there for the night, to keep his eyes open. So the poor bastard kept his eyes open. When he hadn't come back by five o'clock, his wife called the local precinct. They found him in the doctor's second floor study-office. He'd been shot through the head like the others."

"Oh, brother!" Quist said.

"Just to add to the gaiety of nations," Kreevich said, "ballistics has just reported to me that the same gun was used—Dr. Martine, the nurse, Gamage. So, the same killer. Now listen to me, Julian. Your friend Craven had better show up, and damned quick! He's just about run out of time."

PART TWO

1

It was hard to believe that Bart Craven, in his secret hideout, wherever it might be, was not in touch with what was going on in the world. Radio news programs, going round and round every twenty minutes, had reported on the progress, if any, in the police work on the murder of Dr. Martine and his live-in nurse. Now, with a new day brightening the streets, the tempo of excitement was stepped way up. There was a new murder, under the same roof, committed by the same killer.

"Bart has to be checking on news programs from time to time," Quist said, over an early coffee Lydia had hurried to make for him. "With this second violence he has to know he can't stay hidden."

"You can't have it all three ways at once," Lydia said.

"Three ways?"

"If he's guilty, as Mark thinks he may be, of course he's watching, listening, reading every speck there is about the case. If he's trying to play detective, then he's truly off his rocker and not paying attention to anything but his own music, wherever that comes from. If he's the Bart Craven I think I know, then he's holed up somewhere, trying to fight back a renewed hope that there may be something about Maureen. He can't do that and listen to all the chatter about the murders. He isn't listening to news. He's battling with his own emotions. It's one of those ways, Julian, not all three. I buy the last one."

Quist sipped his coffee, frowning. "I'd like to buy that one, too," he said. "But one way or another we've got to find him. I'm going to get to George Strock. He's an expert at locating missing people." He started for the phone.

"Julian?"

"Yes, love?"

"If he turns up, not guilty, as I believe he will, will the party people still support him for the Senate—Graves, Molloy, Senator Metzger?"

"It's going to depend a lot on how the news media, and through them the general public, react in the next twenty-four hours," Quist said. "People should have forgotten and forgiven Chappaquiddick, a tragic accident, but they never have or will. You and I and the rest of our people have got to sell the public something digestible, and in a hurry."

Lieutenant Kreevich's digestion wasn't improved by what was revealed in the Martine house on East Thirty-eighth Street. Gamage, the dead caretaker, had carried a large key ring with a couple of dozen keys linked to it hooked to his belt. There wasn't a forced door anywhere in the house, front or back. The basement door was unlocked. There had been a faint sprinkle of snow in the early hours and Gamage's trail along the back alley to that door was clearly marked. Apparently no one else had come or gone that way.

Gamage's hysterical wife indicated that was the way he would have gone to let himself in.

"Let himself in with the key on his ring," Sergeant Kaminski told Kreevich. He'd arrived ahead of the lieutenant. He was Kreevich's top assistant. "Closed the door but didn't lock it. It was cold outside. Couple of puddles of water inside. Must have been snow off his shoes that melted. Looks like he went up the back stairs to the second floor where he'd seen the light. There he was confronted by the murderer who shot him right between the eyes. Just one shot, like the two earlier ones."

"Bastard knows how to use a gun," Kreevich said. He found himself thinking that Bart Craven had been trained to use weapons long ago in Korea. He couldn't shake the thought of Craven. "How did he come and go—the killer?"

"Not by way of the back alley," Kaminski said. He was a tall, dark man with a solemn, humorless look. "The only other door is the office door." The Sergeant shrugged. "Foot cop on the beat went to that door a half a dozen times during the night—just to check. Two cops in a patrol car stopped each time around, every half-hour, got out, went to the door to see if everything was okay. Snow was light, melted fast. When it was tramped over like that, it left a mess. We're trying to pick up some clear prints, but there really aren't any."

"To begin with, he had to get in," Kreevich said.

"You have to think a key," Kaminski said. "No sign of anything being forced, no scratches that would indicate someone tried to pick a lock. There's one thing, Lieutenant, that may explain it."

"Do I have to beg for it?" Kreevich asked.

"No, sir. I just finished talking to the people at the

precinct morgue. Martine's body is there, with all the belongings they found on him. Fifty-odd dollars in cash, a wallet with driver's license and credit cards, a small address book, a handkerchief. No keys, Lieutenant. A man usually carries keys: house key, car keys. There were cabinets in his office containing medicines, drugs. No key for those cabinets. My guess is . . ."

"The murderer took Martine's keys after he'd killed the doctor, planning to come back?"

"Something like that," Kaminski said.

"He could pretty well time the foot cop and the patrol car. Come in during a gap between visits, leave the same way."

"When you get a look at the rest of the house, Lieutenant, you'll know why he had to come back," Kaminski said. "It must have taken a couple of hours to do the damage that's been done here."

"Damage" was an understatement. Every drawer in every bureau and highboy and desk in the house had been emptied, contents scattered on the floor. Cigarette boxes, Julia Prentiss's jewel case had been emptied onto table tops. Clothes had been taken out of closets, pockets searched. Beds torn apart, bedding scattered. The desk in Ruth Taylor's reception room was a shambles, drawers emptied. Stacks of folders had been taken from the files, papers tossed anywhere. Dr. Martine's consulting room had been taken apart; the only things left relatively undisturbed were the supplies of medicines and drugs. Those cabinets had been opened, suggesting another key, but the contents had, Kreevich guessed, just been moved around like checkers on a board, not swept out onto the floor.

"The jewelry upstairs, the supply of drugs here," Kaminski said, "would be worth a small fortune on the street. It wasn't just robbery, Lieutenant. This guy was looking for one specific thing. Looks like he may not have found it. He was still at work on the second floor when Gamage interrupted him. I wonder what the hell it could have been?"

Kreevich's mouth was a straight, hard line. He wondered if it could have been something that could have told Bart Craven what had happened to Maureen seven years ago.

He made that suggestion some time later to Quist, who had taken advantage of his friendship with the Homicide man to arm himself for what was going to be a rough time with the press, and perhaps an even rougher time with Bart Craven's political friends. Quist could almost see Paul Graves heading for the lifeboats, deserting the ship. Kreevich wasn't actually doing his friend a favor by admitting him to the house on Thirty-eighth Street. Finding Bart Craven was now an essential part of his case, and Quist had direct contacts with most of the people close to Craven.

The two men actually stood talking in the narrow entrance hall inside the front door. An army of Homicide cops and technicians had taken over the rest of the building, searching for fingerprints, any kind of insignificant clue the killer may have left behind him. Kreevich, who was riding harder than ever on his Craven theory, put it on the line.

"I say your friend Craven came here to see Martine, whether in answer to a phone call, or because he imagined or knew that Martine had something that would lead him to Maureen."

"She's dead," Quist said. "She has to be dead."

"Something that would tell Craven how, when, where," Kreevich said. "He and Martine argued in that consulting room and Craven pulled out his gun and shot the doctor, and the nurse, who would have been an incriminating witness. Why he didn't search the house then I can't tell you. Perhaps he thought the shots could have been heard. Perhaps he was afraid some last patient might walk in on the scene. The doctor and his nurse were dressed for business. I say he took the doctor's keys, left, hid the keys and the gun somewhere in case he might be searched, then called us, thus apparently clearing himself. After we'd finished our business, he could come back and search at leisure."

"And he waited a whole day?"

"He had to. We were in and out for almost a day and a half, before we shut up the house last night. He had to wait."

"Knowing that you might find what he wanted so badly?"

"Knowing that we hadn't found it, whatever it is, or we'd have been talking about it."

"How did Bart know what to look for?" Quist asked. "For seven years he hasn't known what to look for or where to look for it. For six years George Strock, an experienced investigator, hasn't known what to look for or where to look for it."

Kreevich stayed stubbornly with it. "So maybe Dr. Martine did call him. Maybe it was, as we thought in the beginning, an intended blackmail. Martine tells Craven, when he arrives, what it is he's got. He tells Craven how much it will cost him to get it. Craven pulls out his gun and pow, pow!"

"That suggests that whatever Martine had, Bart wouldn't have wanted it made public."

"Of course it does." Kreevich held his lighter to a cigarette. "You must have thought about all the possible solutions to the Maureen Craven case," he said.

"And came up with the same one you and everyone

else came up with years ago. She was killed and disposed of by a mugger or a sex nut."

"Now hold onto your hat, Julian. Has it never occurred to you that Bart Craven might have killed his own wife and disposed of her? Acted out his grief charade for seven years just so no one would look his way? If that's what Martine had on him . . ."

"Oh, for Christ's sake, Mark!"

"You think that's crazy because you know the guy, like him," Kreevich said. "Well, I don't know him, Julian, so I have no reason to like or not like him. He's just a piece in a puzzle to me. Turn it one way and it fits; turn it another way and it fits. What do I, a police officer, know about Bartley J. Craven? One, he's a public figure with a good record, planning to run for office. Two, he's a man who suffered a severe trauma seven years ago and has acted a little eccentrically ever since."

"Is it eccentric for him to want to find the answer to what happened to his wife?" Quist asked.

"Of course not. But it's a touch eccentric for him not to accept the verdict the police gave him. It's a touch eccentric for him to keep a private detective on the payroll for *six years!* It's eccentric for a mature man to disappear periodically, leaving no clue to where he is with people who count on him—his secretary, his housekeeper, his friends, his professional associates. It is particularly eccentric for him to choose this moment, when he's at the center of a criminal investigation, to pull one of these disappearances, to talk, wildly, about finding the killer himself. To me, a cop who doesn't know him, has no reason to like him or not like him, all that comes out eccentric; comes out a man who isn't entirely in balance, Julian. I have to travel down his street before I can write him off."

"Because you don't have any other street to travel?"

"Perhaps," Kreevich conceded. "But I can't wait for something else to turn up before I check out what I have."

"You can destroy the man's life by making him a public suspect," Quist said.

"I know that. That's why you're here, friend, listening to me whistle my tune. I'll give you a few hours to find him. Talk to the women—the secretary and the house-keeper. Maybe they'll have remembered something they haven't thought to tell us about where he goes on these walk-outs. Maybe he's dropped a hint sometime over these seven years that they'll remember, now that they know he's in big trouble. Talk to George Strock. What would he have done if he'd come up with something about Maureen during one of Craven's fade-outs? It's hard to believe that a man who was so desperate for information about his missing wife would be out of touch with the man who was looking for her. Talk to your friend Jack Milburn. He's been close to Craven since they were kids. Did you have secret hiding places when you were a kid that you might have shared with a best friend? Those people are Craven's best chance to save his hide at the moment, Julian. If I haven't located him by—by this afternoon, I'll put out a general alarm for him and the whole damn world will know what I'm thinking."

It wasn't too difficult for Quist to get those people Kreevich had named together. All of them were waiting near phones for some word. Rachel Hoyt hadn't wanted to leave Craven's apartment on Gramercy Park. He might call there. So the others gathered in Craven's library, and Quist told them what Kreevich was think-

78

ing and planning to do if Bart didn't appear, almost at once.

There were varying degrees of outrage from Dilys, and Rachel, and Jack Milburn. George Strock, the elderly private eye, helped to bring the others down to earth.

"We all know Bart," he said, "so we all know what the lieutenant is suggesting is absurd."

"And how!" Jack Milburn said.

"But if I were a dispassionate cop on the case, I would be thinking just as he is thinking," Strock said. "He has no other leads to follow, and Bart's walking out this way has to make him think he's dealing with a man who's way off base."

But this is nothing new for Bart," Milburn said. "Ever since Maureen disappeared he's chosen to isolate himself like this from time to time."

"Let me ask you something, George," Quist said to the detective. "If you'd come up with something about Maureen along the way, during one of these self-chosen isolations, how would you have reached Bart to tell him?"

Strock took off his wire-rimmed glasses, blew on them, and wiped them clean with a linen handkerchief. "I had a number of ways," he said. "I had this number here, of course. I had his office number. I also had Miss Johns' home phone, and Mr. Milburn's home phone."

"That suggests Bart thought one of them would know where he was," Quist said.

"I think you misunderstood me, Mr. Quist," Strock said. "Bart didn't give me those numbers. I dug them out for myself. I knew that he sometimes took off —never told me where. I was sure one of these others would know where he was. But, God help me, I never had any reason to call. I never found anything, not even anything that entitled me to a guess."

"Bart never gave you any procedure for reaching him when he took off somewhere?"

"He never told me when he was taking off," Strock said. "But you know I wasn't in constant touch with him. I was all over the country on other cases, out of the city here, weeks on end. I'd always call him when I got back to town—only to tell him that none of the Missing Persons Bureaus I'd contacted in other cities had found anything helpful. Sometimes I couldn't reach him, but Mrs. Hoyt would tell me he'd be back in a day or so. Then he'd call me."

"You didn't think these absences were odd?"

"Not really," Strock said. "It wasn't often. You don't always expect to find a man at home. He could have been visiting friends in the country. I never gave it a thought—until a little while ago. Then Mrs. Hoyt told me what was really cooking. You see, I never had anything important to tell him so there was no pressure to reach him." Strock shook his head. "I was almost glad sometimes that he wasn't available."

"You told George what was cooking?" Quist asked Rachel Hoyt.

She nodded. "It was very hard to take," she said. "He never told any of us that he was going anywhere. The first few times, when he didn't come home, I called Dilys, I called Jack. They didn't know anything. We were frightened at first, but he always came back after a day or two."

"With an explanation?"

"Not really. I told him what he did was his own business, but it was unkind of him to leave us worried and frightened. He said there came times when he just

80

had to be alone with his problems. I said that was reasonable, but he could at least let us know when he was going off by himself. 'I don't know myself, Rachel,' he said. 'I start out for the office and I find that it's a day when I just can't face the world.' One day, when he was gone again, Mr. Strock came here to see him. I was beside myself, wondering what to do for Bart, how to help. So I told Mr. Strock about the—the disappearances."

"I wasn't much help," Strock said. "I thought I understood what was eating the man, but I didn't know how to help him—except to find his wife, or facts about what had happened to her. I've been a flop at that."

"Did he take a bag, clothes, anything with him when he went off on one of these jaunts?" Quist asked.

"No," Rachel said. "He'd start out, just like any other day, and then not show up."

"And you, Dilys," Quist said. "How did he explain his absences from the office?"

"After that first blow-up with Rachel he spelled it out for me," Dilys said in her little girl voice. "If he didn't show up at the office by ten o'clock, I would know he wasn't coming and should cancel his appointments. I was to say, if anyone insisted, that he was out of town and I didn't know how to reach him."

"This wasn't a once-a-week thing, you know," Jack Milburn said. "It was once every two to three months. There isn't any pattern to it."

"Did you never have it out with him?" Quist asked.

"Oh, sure, the first few times," Milburn said. "I tried being angry. I tried kidding him about it; suggested he had a gal hidden away somewhere. That turned him grim. There'd never be any other woman in his life but Maureen."

Quist looked around at four unhappy faces. "Rachel,

81

you and Jack have been close to him all his life. Dilys, you've worked for him for ten years."

"And eight months," she said.

"George, you've been on his payroll for almost seven years. You four people are closer to him than anyone else anywhere. You make it sound as if there was some kind of a wall between you and Bart."

"Only after Maureen," Jack Milburn said. "He was fourteen years old, I was twelve, when we first met at school. We shared everything, jokes, secrets, everything. We grew from kids into men. Saw each other almost every day through college. I don't think there was anything I didn't know about how he felt, about his career, about judgments he had to make. I worked in his office. I traveled abroad with him on government business. I don't think any two men have ever been closer."

"And then he married Maureen," Quist said.

"Of course that changed things," Milburn said, "but not unhappily. It did so much for him, opened him wide up. If he had been a little shy, a little unsure of himself along the way, he was now a vigorous, self-confident, whole human being. And then bang! It was all over. He seemed to draw down a shutter between himself and those of us who were close to him. It was as though he were determined to make sure we'd never see what he was really thinking, really feeling. Express sympathy for him and he'd slam the door in your face. It's been like walking on eggs with him for seven long years!" Milburn's voice had grown unsteady and he turned away.

Quist brought his fist down on the arm of his chair. "But where is he *now*? If we don't find him and pull together this thing is going to destroy him. George, this is your world—a missing person."

82

"I don't know where to start," Strock said. "Not and find him in a few hours."

"Then God help him," Quist said.

Getting those four people together had seemed to Quist like the best way of dealing with his major problem, which was time. Talking to each one separately could drag on and on. Together, one of them might say "remember the time when . . .," which would stir a memory that would produce something, some small incident that would provide a crumb of evidence, an insignificant clue to where Bart went for his periods of isolation. The get-together had brought up nothing and used up about an hour and a half of precious time.

Dilys went back to Bart's office, Milburn to his own apartment. There was the clinging hope that one of them might hear from Bart at those places. Quist stayed behind with Rachel Hoyt and George Strock.

"I'd like it, George, if you'd take this on as a case, top of your list," Quist said. "My firm will pay your fee."

"You don't have to pay me," Strock said. "I think of him as my friend."

"I want to hire you, George. That means I can call on you for whatever."

"If you want," Strock said. "But when I walk out of here I just wet my finger and test the wind. Frankly, I don't know where to begin."

"If we don't find Bart or he doesn't show up in a very short time his political career is over, he's had it," Quist said. "There may be a way to stall Kreevich, however. A taxi driver."

"I don't get it," Strock said.

"According to Bart, he got a phone call from Dr. Martine about eight-thirty, twenty minutes to nine. He was in this room, undressed—pajamas and dressing gown. Martine told him what he had to offer. Bart had to get dressed. Let's say ten minutes. So sometime between eight-thirty and ten minutes to nine he was down on the street, looking for a taxi. He found one and was driven up to Thirty-eighth Street. Got there a few minutes after nine, walked into the office, waited a few minutes, then looked in the consulting room. He found the murdered doctor and his nurse, went out to the reception room and called the police. If that's the way it was, George, it will make Kreevich think twice. For his case to stick, Bart must have gone there earlier, had a lot more time to kill, to cover his tracks, to take Martine's keys, to dispose of his gun and those keys before the cops came. They've looked for the taxi driver to help verify Bart's story. No dice. Kreevich thinks the driver hasn't come forward because he didn't enter the ride on his trip sheet. Short run, no gas that he wouldn't have used just cruising. So he makes three or four bucks."

"The meter?" Rachel asked.

"He may not have thrown his flag. In Bart's state of mind he wouldn't have noticed. At any rate, until he turns up we can't ask him. But you might find the driver, George. We could make it worth his while to testify for Bart. Drivers have a regular cruising routine, don't they? There must be drivers who hang around this part of town at night."

"Could be a guy coming back from a trip, not his regular area at all," Strock said.

"But you're not a cop, George. You might be able to get wind of something the police couldn't smell out. The driver might talk to you, if you could find him and dangle a few bucks under his nose."

"It's at least a place to begin," Strock said. "I'm on my way."

"But it's got to happen so fast, George!" Quist said. Quist and Rachel watched the little detective leave. It was a slim hope, but a hope.

"It's so unfair," Rachel said.

Quist glanced at her. Forty years of caring for a man on an almost daily basis. Family couldn't have been closer.

"Bart has put himself behind the eight ball by choosing to take off," Quist said. "Lieutenant Kreevich has no choice but to play the cards the way they're dealt to him."

"Oh, I understand that. I wasn't saying the police were being unfair. It's just that Bart's whole life has been twisted and made unbearable by events he did nothing to create, make happen. Mostly, in this life, we are punished for something we have done. Bart has been repeatedly punished by events he didn't make for himself. He was twelve years old when his parents died, and he was left alone. He wasn't responsible for what had happened to him, but he had to live with it."

"That's when you came into his life?"

"Just by chance," Rachel said, looking away from Quist. "The trustee for Bart's father's will was the family lawyer. It happened that my mother, a widow, was that lawyer's secretary. Someone was needed to look out for young Bart on a day-to-day basis—just a temporary arrangement. I was just out of junior college, looking for a job. My mother suggested I could handle things till something permanent was arranged. It worked well. Bart liked me. Could you guess why, Mr. Quist? Because he cried quite a lot, and I wouldn't let him be embarrassed by it. He had a right to tears."

"Wise young woman," Quist said. "Tears are often therapy if you don't get to like the sound of the music."

"Arrangements were made to send Bart away to

85

school and I supposed my job was over," Rachel said. "But old Mr. Ogilvy, the lawyer, was a good, sensitive man. Bart wasn't just going away to school, he was being cut off from the world he'd known. There was plenty of money, so Mr. Ogilvy decided to keep the town house, where Bart had grown up, open, with me in residence. The boy would always know he had a place of his own to go to. I suppose you would call it a luxury for me. I had very little to do to earn my salary during school terms. But Bart came home for holidays, Christmas, Easter. In the summer the Cravens had always gone to a place in the Berkshires. They had a cottage there, outside of Stockbridge. Bart wanted to go there for the summer, and I went along to take care of him. It was suddenly permanent."

"What about friends? Weren't there any uncles or aunts?"

"Mr. Craven, Bart's father, had a sister. She lives in Arizona somewhere. She was never really interested in the boy. She dutifully sent him Christmas and birthday presents. He went to visit her once. It didn't work. There was no one on his mother's side. That first year he brought Jack Milburn home for the holidays. It was the beginning of the only solid relationship he'd ever had—except Maureen. A lot of people have liked and admired him, all over the world, but I don't think anyone has ever really been close to him except Jack and Maureen."

"And you," Quist said.

"My mother died when I was twenty-five," Rachel said. "The trustees kept me on. When Bart was twenty-one—I was almost thirty—he came into the management of his own affairs. I gave him the chance of telling me to go peddle my papers. He wouldn't hear of it. He sold the town house—it was much too large for just two

86

people. He bought this apartment. It's a co-op, you know. We—we've been here ever since."

"Thirty years."

"Yes."

"Then he brought his bride here. That worked out all right for you, Rachel?"

"She was a wonderful girl," Rachel said. She took a deep breath to fight off the quaver in her voice. "Gay, fun, laughing—and she cared for him so much. I thought at last he really had a life. It was as if he were transformed. He was suddenly outgoing, his almost painful shyness disappeared. The place was full of guests, friends. I supposed Maureen would want to make her own choice about someone to run the establishment for her. She wouldn't hear of my going. 'Bart loves you,' she said."

"And you love him?"

"Of course I do! He was like my own child, you know?"

"He's an attractive man," Quist said. "Not too young for you, Rachel, if you were interested."

She looked at him as if he didn't make sense. "I took care of him. That was my job. Maureen made a whole new world for him. That's what I meant about 'unfair,' Mr. Quist. It was perfect. He did everything to make it perfect. And then, through no fault of his, she was gone, in that cruel fashion. Now, today, he's in trouble because of something he had nothing to do with. He fulfilled his responsibilities as a good citizen, and then, because it revived an old agony, he took off to get himself pulled together, and his future is in danger. I've prayed he would run for the Senate, get elected, have a life again. It's just not fair, Mr. Quist."

"And he never indicated to you where he went on these times away?" Quist asked.

"No, and I never pressed him about it. If he'd wanted me to know, he'd have told me. I knew why, of course. He's a very, very private man, Mr. Quist. He has to work out his own problems in his own way."

"He needs someone to tell him how deep a hole he's digging for himself," Quist said. "You mentioned some kind of a summer cottage in the Berkshires —Stockbridge, was it? Does he still have that?"

"He still owns it," Rachel said. "He and Maureen went there for five summers. I don't think he's been back since—since she went away."

"But you don't know? He could be there? He has clothes there? A perfect place to be by himself, isn't it?"

"When he first started disappearing, seven years ago, that's the first place I thought of," Rachel said. "When I tried, the phone had been disconnected. I knew some people in the village, casually, from summers there. I asked them to check out the cottage. Bart wasn't there, not the first few times. I decided that wasn't where he was going. He never said anything that made me think he'd been up there in Massachusetts."

"Could you try again now? Reach your friends there?"

"Of course. It will probably take an hour or so to reach my friends, have them drive out to the cottage, and report back."

"If he's gone there and we didn't look we'd never forgive ourselves," Quist said.

2

Lieutenant Kreevich was not a man who refused to turn a problem over and over in an effort to find the proper handle. He had laid out a pretty good case against Bart Craven for Quist. The fact that the man had disappeared lent weight to it. But it wasn't impossible that things had happened just exactly as Bart Craven had described them: a phone call from the stranger, Dr. Martine; the promise of news about Maureen, gone for so long; his dressing, going uptown in a taxi, and finding two people murdered.

"Assume, for the moment, every word of it is true," Kreevich said to Sergeant Kaminski. The two detectives were sitting in a coffee shop on Lexington Avenue, not a block from Dr. Martine's Thirty-eighth Street house.

"Could be, of course," Kaminski said. He was dark, quiet, a perfect sounding board for the intense Kreevich.

"So we have Dr. Martine making the call at, say, eight thirty-five in the evening. Craven throws on some clothes, flags the first taxi he sees on the street, comes up here. About thirty-five minutes, let's say. He stays in the walk-in office, waiting for someone to show. After a while he goes into the consulting room and finds two dead people. He hangs onto his nerve, goes back into the reception room and calls us. He's been involved for forty minutes. His call reached the Fifteenth Precinct at nine-fifteen."

"If what he says is all true."

"Right." Kreevich lit one of his inevitable cigarettes, his bright eyes narrowed against the smoke.

"So we're looking for a third person, a Mr. X," Kaminski said.

"Or a Mrs. X," Kreevich said. "A lady with a mangled face who chooses that moment to get even for a surgical mistake."

"But if Craven is telling the truth, Dr. Martine did say he knew what had happened to Maureen Craven seven years ago."

"Two things not connected," Kreevich said. "Or Mrs. X could be . . .?"

"Oh, wow!" Kaminski said. "Maureen Craven is alive?"

"We don't know, for a fact, that she's dead," Kreevich said.

"That *is* a dream-up, Lieutenant!"

"I know."

"Missing Persons looked for her for months," Kaminski said. "George Strock, a good man, has been looking for her for six years."

"I know."

Kaminski shook his head. "I have to stay with the idea that Craven tried to sell us a bill of goods, Lieutenant. I think he's known all along what happened to his wife, and when Martine indicated that he knew what that was, Craven went there and shot him."

"Why?"

"You said it, some time earlier on," Kaminski said. "He came home from a trip abroad a couple of days early. Surprise! Only he got the surprise. Found his wife in the hay with somebody else? Could be."

"Kills her, disposes of her body, and then spends

seven years pretending to look for her? Hires a detective to find her?"

"He knows the detective won't find her," Kaminski said.

"So we have a seven-year-old murder and three one-day-old murders, all connected," Kreevich said.

"Could be. Craven steals Martine's keys. He can't search the house then. Another patient may walk in any minute. He'll come back later—and did."

"Why call us? Why get himself involved at all? He could have just walked out after he shot the doctor and his nurse, not called us at all, not called attention to himself at all?"

"Taxi driver brought him up here from Gramercy Park. That driver might remember at some point. He could have recognized Craven, a public figure, pictures in the papers and on TV. Craven couldn't risk that coming back at him. Maybe he passed someone in the vestibule of the house as he was going into the walk-in office. Risk of being recognized again he couldn't take. A cool customer, Lieutenant."

"Or a completely innocent man, tangled up in someone else's web. I never thought I'd be looking for clues to today's murder in a seven-year-old past. Let's try on a Mr. X for size."

"You still got the past to deal with," Kaminski said. "If Craven is completely innocent, then Martine *did* call him, *did* say he knew what had happened to Maureen. The past is right up front again, Lieutenant. Introduce a Mr. X who has nothing to do with it. Martine has made his call. He and the Prentiss doll are waiting for Craven. In walks Mr. X with some other axe to grind. Maybe he heard Martine making that famous phone call to Craven, so he knew Craven was on the way. He kills the doctor and the nurse, steals the doctor's keys, waits for the decks to clear so he can come back and search the house for what he wants."

"Which is what?" Kreevich said.

"Don't expect too much from me all at once," Kaminski said.

Kreevich laughed, a bitter little sound. "Maybe we both better turn in our badges, Kam, and take to writing television scripts." He punched out his cigarette in the ash tray on the table. "There's one thing that remains pretty constant, no matter which invention you like. Dr. Claude Martine smells a little rank. If Craven is telling us the truth, then we have to think Martine was up to blackmail or extortion. If Craven is lying and it's something like what we invented, then Martine still smells bad. A man of Craven's reputation, stature, possible future, doesn't commit a double murder unless the screws are being turned on him good. No man or woman, not Craven, or Mr. X, or Mrs. X, comes back a day and a half after murdering two people to search for something unless it's incriminating. Martine was bearing down hard on whoever it was and got paid off more totally than he'd expected." The lieutenant pushed back his chair and stood up. "I want to see the Missing Persons Bureau's final file on Maureen Craven. Get it for me, Kam."

"Right."

"While you're doing that, I want to talk to someone who may be able to give us the real dirt on Dr. Claude Martine."

"The receptionist?"

"I don't think so. But there's a lady somewhere who may be willing to tell us a thing or two; a lady who won a paternity suit against our doctor and who may be wondering where her next month's rent is coming from now that she's heard that Martine won't be paying any more."

Jack Milburn looked surprised when he answered his apartment's doorbell and saw Quist standing outside.

"Julian! Something new?"

Quist shook his head. "I need to talk, Jack," he said.

"Don't we all! Come in."

It was a pleasant, small apartment, looking out on a quiet East Side street. It didn't tell Quist much about the man who was his squash-playing partner at the Athletic Club. A few books, a hi-fi system, a color TV set. Not a place a woman had decorated, made to look like home. It was a place where a man who lived his life somewhere else slept, kept his clothes. There were half a dozen athletic trophies on the mantle over the fireplace. There were several pictures of college teams, twenty-five to thirty years back. Milburn, Quist remembered, had been an All-American halfback in his time. The furniture was out of an expensive department store, nothing antique, just comfortable and solid.

"It's a little early in the day, but would you like a drink?" Milburn asked.

Quist glanced at his watch. It was going on one o'clock. Kreevich would be yelling for results pretty soon.

"I think I'll wait till Bart shows up, or until he doesn't and I decide to get blind," Quist said. He sat down in an upholstered armchair that Milburn indicated. He told Milburn that Rachel was trying to locate Bart in Stockbridge.

"I don't think he's there," Milburn said, frowning. "I don't think he goes anywhere that was once a part of his life with Maureen. He doesn't want any part of anything that reminds him of his life with her."

"And yet everything reminds him of it."

"Yes. I don't suppose there's an hour of any day he doesn't think about her."

"It's as if he's perpetually punishing himself," Quist said. "Did he blame himself for her disappearance in any way at the time?"

Milburn paced restlessly up and down the hearth rug. "I suppose he did, in a way. He took that trip to the Middle East for the State Department, the first time they'd been separated in the five years of their marriage. I suppose he's told himself a thousand times that if he hadn't gone she'd be safe. She'd have been with him. Nothing would have happened to her."

"But if she was mugged on the street, attacked by a sex nut, it could have happened to her anytime she went out on an errand, anytime she went to the hairdresser, or the dentist. I mean, he didn't go everywhere with her."

"No, of course he didn't. But you know how it is; if he'd been here, she might not have gone out at that critical time. It's not justified, not real, but you can see how Bart might feel it."

Quist took one of the long, thin cigars out of the leather case he carried in his breast pocket and lit it.

"What could this Dr. Martine have known about Maureen—after seven years?" he asked.

"I haven't the faintest idea, Julian."

"He could know that Bart is rich and would pay for that kind of information."

"Sure, if he read the papers seven years ago. It was a big deal at the time. Prominent diplomat, former movie star. Pictures of Maureen everywhere. 'If you've seen this woman, call this special number.' A thousand people saw her, except, of course, they didn't, hadn't. Nothing ever proved out. Now, seven years later! It's crazy, you know? Only someone like Bart would fall for it. He's always said that if she were really dead he would know; some instinct would tell him. The poor bastard still dreams that she'll turn up. So there's this phone call, and all his hopes spring to life again. He races up to that house to get the news and the man is dead. No wonder he's taken off to get over it in private."

"Have you ever thought she might be alive, Jack?"

"Hell, yes, the first little stretch of time, the first few weeks. I couldn't believe she was dead, you understand? I'd had dinner with her the night before she disappeared. We went to see *A Little Night Music.* She was so damned alive!"

"You said yesterday that you were in love with her."

"A figure of speech," Milburn said. "Everyone who knew her was in love with her. She was the most fascinating gal I think I ever met."

"And when Bart was in the Middle East you saw a lot of her?"

"My dear Julian, Bart is my best friend. Before he left he asked me to look out for her, make sure she wasn't bored. I suppose I took her out twice a week during the month he was gone, called her on the phone every day. My best friend's wife, that's all it was."

"You introduced them, didn't you? Blind date, Bart told me."

Milburn laughed. "Maybe I should have had my head examined. I handed over the most attractive woman I've ever known to somebody else. I'll tell you how it was. I had a date for dinner with a gal. She wasn't anyone special in my life, just someone who was involved in a real estate deal my office was trying to work out. At the last minute I ran into Bart somewhere —the Athletic Club, as I remember. He was having one of his low spells. He had 'em, you know, long before he met Maureen. I suggested he join us for dinner. He seemed to need company, and he said yes. I called my date and asked her if she had a friend. She did, an attractive English movie actress, who was on her way back to London after making a film in Hollywood. So Bart and I met Maureen that night. Before I could give much thought to how much I'd like to know her really well, the unexpected happened. She and Bart hit it off like you wouldn't believe. Before any of us could even imagine it happening, they were married, just three weeks after they met."

"Good match for her. He is a very rich man."

"That was one of the reassuring things about it," Milburn said. "She wasn't attracted by his money. She'd hit the top in the film business. She had plenty of money."

"But she dropped her career," Quist said. "Twenty-five years old, at the top of the heap, and she quit. Strange, in this day and age of women's lib, separate careers."

"It didn't seem strange at first. She was so much in love. All she cared about was to make him happy." Milburn hesitated. "That last month, when Bart was away and I was seeing her, she talked a little bit about going back to acting. All she had to do was blink an eye and half a dozen of the top producers would have been lined up to sign her. Have you ever seen any of her films?"

"Two, I think—on late TV. She was good."

"She was marvelous," Milburn said.

"And she was thinking of going back?" Quist leaned forward. "Was the marriage going stale, Jack?"

"Oh, God, no," Milburn said. "But—well, you and I talked about it before. No children. I think that's what Maureen dreamed of when they got married—three or four kids, nothing to be concerned about but her home, her husband, her family. I think Bart was urging her to get back to her career. That's seven years ago, Julian, long before he thought of doing anything about himself. He could go wherever she had to go, it wouldn't involve separation. She was thinking seriously about it, I know."

"It didn't go deeper than that? She wasn't looking for a way out of a situation that had soured?"

"Lord, no! Every other word she spoke was love for Bart, concern for Bart. She was proud for him that the government had wanted him to undertake the diplomatic mission in the Middle East. I tell you, Julian, they had to be seen to be believed, those two. So wrapped up in each other. You think Bart is moody, neurotic, overdramatizing his loss? If you'd seen them together, you wouldn't."

Quist glanced at the end of his cigar. It had gone out and he had no taste for it.

"You go round and round in this mess, Jack, and it's like trying to put together a puzzle with a key piece missing," he said. "I keep telling myself that if I knew Bart better I could find him. But you and Rachel have known him most of your lives and you come up empty. I keep thinking there's something about Maureen—if I could put my finger on it the whole thing might make sense."

"For God's sake, Julian, she's been dead for seven years!"

"But Dr. Martine brought her to life again, night before last," Quist said. "You know what Lieutenant Kreevich is thinking? If Bart's telling the truth, he's not telling it all. A phone call from a stranger who says he has information about Maureen."

"After seven years?"

"Right. I'm talking for Kreevich, you understand. Bart goes to Thirty-eighth Street. Martine tells him something about Maureen, something scandalous, something Bart couldn't bear to have revealed. Bart kills the doctor and his nurse, who was present during the revelation. Later, early this morning, Bart goes back to the house to look for the evidence of the scandalous story the doctor had."

Milburn brought his fist down on the mantle so hard the athletic trophies there jumped. "What possible scandal could come to Martine after seven years? If he had it before, why did he wait so long to use it?"

"I don't have an answer, Jack, but I can't stop worrying at it. What do you know about Maureen before she married Bart?"

"For God's sake, man, she was only twenty-five years old. She'd made three British films, I think, and was a big star overnight. She came to Hollywood to make a film—something called *Lonely Boy*. She was on her way back to England when she stopped over in New York, met Bart on that blind date, and that was that."

"But before that meeting," Quist persisted. "A beautiful, vital, exciting girl, a star overnight. There must have been men in her life before Bart. Can there have been some kind of scandal, something that would have made Bart kill Martine to keep it from being made public? I can't imagine what."

Milburn shook his head, emphatically. "A woman who was a film star disappears, mysteriously. Police on both sides of the Atlantic are looking for her, private detective looking for her, a nine-days' wonder in the media. If there was some kind of scandal, how could it have been kept bottled up at the time? She wasn't a Scarsdale housewife; she was a glamorous public figure. Reporters were digging into her life history. If some cheap scandalmonger had something, he'd have approached Bart with it long ago."

"We don't know that he wasn't approached," Quist said. "If there was something bad about Maureen, he wouldn't have told you, or Rachel, or anyone. He would have silenced the scandal peddler, paid him off, something. Now it surfaces again, through Martine. This time Bart is off his rocker."

"It just doesn't add up, Julian," Milburn said. "If you'd known Maureen . . ."

"I wish I had."

"If you had, you'd know how unlikely it was that there were deep, dark secrets in her past. Other men? I don't doubt it. You'd almost have to say it would have been unhealthy if there weren't. She was so damn normal. But when she committed herself to Bart what could it matter? I'd bet my last dollar she had no secrets from him. As for some *big* secret, as I said before, it couldn't have been hidden all these years. She was a public glamor girl."

The person who had searched Dr. Martine's house during the night and early morning hours, the person who had shot and killed Pete Gamage, the superintendent-caretaker, had left everything but his name and address for Kreevich and his Homicide crew to find. He had left fingerprints in room after room. A man who was interested in the doctor's files couldn't have handled the stacks of papers with gloves. His prints were everywhere. Kreevich, who had suggested to Sergeant Kaminski that the killer might be a "Mrs. X," had to back away from that theory. The technicians were quite certain the collection of prints came from a man—"or a giant woman." Homicide's immediate problem was that there were no matching prints in the Police

Department files, and, so far, no identification from the FBI's massive collection in Washington. Kreevich had applied to the Air Force for the fingerprints of Lieutenant Bartley J. Craven who had served in Korea back around 1950.

The other information the killer of the unfortunate Gamage had left behind him was that he was also the murderer of Dr. Martine and Julia Prentiss. Unquestionably the same gun, according to Ballistics.

"Everything but his name and picture!" Kreevich said angrily to Sergeant Kaminski. "Fingerprints that don't match anything, gun we haven't got."

"And we don't know what he was looking for," Kaminski said.

"If it was Craven, he was looking for something about his wife."

"And if it wasn't Craven?"

"If Dr. Martine was a blackmailer and extortionist, there must be something incriminating about other people in the files, in those crates of old records in the basement."

"A month's work," Kaminski said.

"Does that mean we don't try looking?" Kreevich said. "Get some people on it, Max."

One of the cops on duty stuck his head in the door of the reception room where Kreevich and Kaminski were talking.

"A fellow named George Strock is outside, Lieutenant. He says you know him. He's got a guy with him he says you may want to see in connection with the case."

"Bring him in," Kreevich said.

Strock, looking professional behind his wire-rimmed glasses, had a short, stocky black man with him. "I felt you'd want to talk to Charley Brinker, Lieutenant," he said. "He thinks he brought Bart Craven here, night before last."

"What have you been doing, Brinker, waiting for it to hatch?" Kreevich asked, not friendly. "It's been on the radio and TV that we were looking for you."

"There's a small irregularity involved, Lieutenant," Strock said.

"Skimming something off the top from the cab company?" Kreevich asked.

"It's like an everyday thing, Lieutenant," the driver said. "Cost of a taxi ride has gone way up, tips going way down."

"I told Charley you might not have to make a big thing of it, Lieutenant," Strock said. "It would cost him his job."

"It depends on what he tells us," Kreevich said.

"You better tell the lieutenant, Charley," Strock said.

Charley Brinker moistened his lips, uneasily. "I'm doing it for a friend," he said. "That's why I'm here."

Strock gave the lieutenant a wry little smile. "Every once in a while, in my business, there's a miracle," he said. "A couple of years ago I was looking for a missing kid, ran away from home out in Minnesota somewhere. A teen-age girl. They thought she might have flown into New York a couple of days before. I went out to Kennedy, was talking to people out there. I had a picture of the girl. I went out to the hack stand, thinking some cab driver might have seen her. I ran into a violence. Some goon was pistol whipping the taxi driver."

"Trying to rob him," Charley Brinker said.

"I got in the act," Strock said. "I nailed the attacker, turned him over to the cops, and got Charley's friend to the hospital. He was pretty badly beaten up."

"He might of died right there if George hadn't helped him," Brinker said.

"This morning Quist and I thought, if we could find the driver who brought Craven here night before last, it might help clear him. Needle-in-a-haystack kind of thing. I went to the guy I had helped at Kennedy. Because he owed me, he got a real network of cabbies asking questions, looking for Craven's driver. That was the rare miracle, Lieutenant. They found him. Charley Brinker here is the man. He talked to me when he might not have talked to everyone."

"So talk to me now, Charley," Kreevich said.

"I had a trip a little after eight o'clock," Brinker said. "Fare wanted to go to an off-Broadway theater down on Second Avenue. It was near the end of my time on duty, about eight-thirty. I figured to head into the garage, but there was time for one more fare if he didn't want to go out to an airport or up to Yonkers or some place like that. I started north and cut west across Twenty-first Street. It runs on the north side of Gramercy Park. This guy comes out of an apartment building there, right out into the center of the street, waving his arms at me. I told him I was heading in. 'It's an emergency,' he told me. 'Just a short way, Thirty-eighth Street, just west of Lexington.' That was on my way so I took him."

"Just after eighty-thirty?"

Brinker shook his head. "Nearer nine. You see, after I dropped my last fare at the theater, I stopped in a lunchroom for a cup of coffee. I drove this guy up town. I had a feeling I knew him from somewhere, but I couldn't place him. We get people like that all the time, movie actors, television actors. They're familiar when you see 'em, but you don't quite place 'em. Well, I let him out at this building. He handed me a five dollar bill, waved at me to keep the change, and ran in here."

102

"And you didn't enter the ride on your trip sheet?"

Brinker nodded. "It had been a bad night for tips. It was five bucks clear. I wouldn't have to account for gas. I was on my way in. Later—well, I heard what had happened here. I thought, Jesus, maybe I took the murderer there. But the story he told sounded fair enough, right time, right everything. So I kept my mouth shut until George's friend came asking, and I told him."

"You realized afterward that your passenger was Bart Craven?"

Brinker nodded. "He's been on a couple of talk shows—politicians and like that."

"I hope what Charley's told you helps Bart," Strock said.

"It would help him a hell of a lot more if he'd just show up!" Kreevich said. Actually he felt the foundation beginning to crumble under the only solid theory he had. If part of Bart's story was true, why not the rest of it?

"Ten years and eight months, you told me," Quist said to Dilys Johns. "So you came to work for Bart after he was married to Maureen."

Bart's office in the Seldon Building on Park Avenue South was only a stone's throw from his apartment. A stranger, looking at the outer door, would have had no idea what went on behind it. It bore, simply, the legend BARTLEY J. CRAVEN. What kind of business was transacted there wasn't indicated. It didn't invite strangers or salesmen.

There wasn't much to the suite, but what there was of it was elegant. The outer office, Dilys's domain, looked more like an executive's. There was no visible typewriter, no filing cabinets, no office machinery of any sort. It was a place to "receive" people; a carved, Florentine desk and chair for Dilys, two comfortable upholstered armchairs, separated by a low coffee table, facing the desk. If there was typing or copying to be done, there must be another room for it.

A heavy oak door to the left of Dilys's desk opened into Bart's office. Quist had seen it on an earlier visit to discuss the possible political campaign. It was more like the library in a rich man's home than an office; books from floor to ceiling, except for space on the west wall for two large windows that opened out onto Park Avenue. Sitting at his flat-topped desk, Bart could swing around in his swivel desk chair and look out at the passing traffic. He was, Quist had thought at the time, and later when he'd seen the library in the apartment, a man who read omnivorously. Except for an encyclopedia, these were not sets of books, unloaded by a salesman to fill up shelves. These were books that had been read, handled, enjoyed. Quist guessed that Bart kept what he admired, enjoyed, or thought useful in his need for knowledge about the governments and the countries of a complex world. History was important to Bart, so were the laws of his own land and of other lands. He was a man who studied his subject, and who might be better equipped for political office than one in a thousand. Quist was pleased when he first made that assessment. He had to believe in the talent, the business, the product that he promoted. Julian Quist Associates was the success it was because it didn't promote fakes or phonies. After first meeting Bart, in the man's own setting, listening to him talk about the party, the Senate, the world walking a tightrope between war and peace, Quist told himself, "I could vote for this man." That day, that first day, he thought he was looking at a man of

104

experience, with skills, who had lived through a dark tragedy and come through it in one piece.

Today he wasn't so sure. A man who dropped out of sight periodically and without warning, a man who could shut out his friends and the people who cared for him, leave them in a state of anxiety about his safety, his health and happiness, wasn't all that stable. He enjoyed his suffering too much, Quist thought. He could be too careless of the feelings of people like Rachel Hoyt and Dilys, who had to hide their concerns, keep their mouths shut, or be fired. Maybe, Quist thought, he couldn't vote for Bart, but neither could he stand by and watch Kreevich feed an innocent man into a meat grinder. He couldn't believe, without a hell of a lot more evidence than Kreevich had, that Bart Craven was the cold-blooded murderer of three people.

Dilys Johns sat at her desk in the outer office, looking as if she were fighting to keep from flying into pieces. Nice eyes, Quist thought, frightened now; a generous mouth, drawn straight and thin. Quist guessed that this was a woman in love, terrified, not for herself, but for her man. He didn't pressure her, but he was still on the trail of Maureen. There must be something in the life of that long-gone woman that would throw light into some of the dark corners.

"They had been married for a little over a year when I came to work for Bart," Dilys said. She gave Quist a tight smile. "You may think it's not respectful for me to call him by his first name, but that's the way he wanted it. The people who worked directly for him—Rachel and I—were too close to him, too much like family, no secrets, to be formal."

"You say 'no secrets', but we're living with one now. Where is he?"

"I know. I mean, I know we're living with a secret. I don't know where he is."

"You're used to not knowing—you and Rachel and Jack Milburn. It's hard for me to take."

"I'm a little different than Rachel or Jack," she said.

I'll bet you are, Quist thought. You're in love with him.

"They knew him, intimately and well, before —Maureen," she said. "They knew him as a young boy, crushed by the death of his parents, shy, introverted. When I came to work for him he was in full bloom. Like the song in *Carousel*—'June Is Bustin' Out All Over.' He was a marvelous, spirited, outgoing, charming guy. I never saw the dark side of him, Mr. Quist. He was so damned happy."

"You got to know Maureen?"

"Yes—in a way. He brought her here to see where he worked. He was so proud of her! He showed her off like a kid. I—I was surprised by her."

"Oh?"

"She was a movie star! I'd seen her films. There was one that came out after they were married—*Lonely Boy*. She was marvelously good. She'd just finished making that when they met. What I mean is, you expect some side, or showing off, or fancy stuff from a person like that. She had none. She was just a very nice woman married to a very nice man. She would drop in here when he was out. 'Did I know something he needed, something he wanted, something she couldn't guess?' And he—almost every day he'd tell me something witty she'd said. 'Isn't that marvelous?' he'd say. I never knew two people so wrapped up in each other."

Quist smiled at Dilys. "You were jealous of her?"

"No, not then, Mr. Quist. Not till long after she was

gone. I've seen the question in your eyes when you look at me. Am I in love with Bart? The answer is yes! Yes, yes, yes! Damn! Hell!" She looked down at her hands which were clenched tightly in front of her. "I suppose I was in love with him right after I started to work for him. But it was just a schoolgirl's crush for an older man who, with a brilliant wife, didn't know I was alive —except as an efficient machine in his office. But after she'd been gone a long time, two, three years, I let myself hope that I could fill the void for him."

"It didn't work?"

"It didn't work. It won't ever work. He's still in love with her."

Quist hesitated. "Did either of them ever talk to you about the fact there were no children?"

"She did. I think she confided in me because I was a woman, because I was devoted to Bart, because she knew I'd cut my tongue out before I'd say anything that could hurt them."

"So she confided—what?"

"I think she thought it must be some lack in her," Dilys said. "In a way, she was a stranger here in New York. They'd both consulted Dr. Janeway. He's Bart's doctor. He's something of an old fogy, I think. He'd told them not to be impatient, everything would work out. She wanted to know if I knew a good gynecologist who'd give her a straight answer."

"And did you know one?"

"Yes. She went to see him. I don't know what he told her. She never mentioned it to me again. But I thought she must have found out it was not her fault."

"It wasn't Dr. Martine?"

"Good God, no! I—I never heard of him till yesterday. The man I sent her to is Dr. George Firchild."

107

"We've got to find Bart, Dilys," Quist said.

"He'll be back," she said. "He always comes back after one of these spells."

"This time he could wait too long," Quist said.

"You don't think for a single minute that Bart . . .?"

"No, I don't, Dilys. But the moment any hint of this hits the street—and the press boys are panting for something—good-bye politics, good-bye future, good-bye the works."

"Oh, my God!" Dilys covered her face with her hands.

"How much do you know about Bart's finances?" Quist asked after a moment.

"Quite a bit," she said, looking up. "I wrote checks for him, paid household bills, kept a sort of running account for him. He hates figures."

"I was thinking more of the source of his income. How rich is he, Dilys?"

"Rich," she said. "There's a folder, locked in his desk drawer in the other room, which contains a record of all his assets: stocks, bonds, properties he owns, companies of which he is a director or in which he has an important interest. I can't recite it for you, Mr. Quist, but I can tell you he's worth a good many millions of dollars."

"Perfect sucker for an extortionist," Quist said. He stood up. "What about Maureen's money?"

Dilys gave him a blank look. "What money?"

"She was a rich woman when they met," Quist said, "making a top star's salary."

"I never heard anything mentioned about her money," Dilys said. "They'd been married about fifteen or sixteen months when I came on the scene. If there were arrangements for her money, I never heard about them."

"It's not very sensible," Quist said. "I need to find

Bart; I need to get Mark Kreevich off his back if his political prospects are to stay alive—and yet I find myself constantly looking for something in the story of woman who disappeared seven years ago!"

"That's because that creepy doctor brought her back to life—for Bart, for all of us. But I'll tell you something, Mr. Quist. Every single possible stone has been turned over in the last seven years—by the police, by George Strock, by Bart himself. There isn't any other answer but murder, a quick disposal of the body, and luck on the side of the killer that it was never found."

"You're thinking of just a mugger, a street violence?"

"She had no enemies."

"She could have had," Quist said. "Some jealous woman, a stagehand or an actor who thought he'd been treated badly. People in public positions, like a movie star, can make private enemies and not even know it."

"But seven years of searching for just that sort of thing, Mr. Quist?"

He was at the door, his hand on the knob. "The money thing still intrigues me, Dilys. Bart will have the answer, of course. She had to have money. Did she pool it with his? Is it in a separate account somewhere? Has it been used since she disappeared?"

Dilys's eyes widened. "What are you suggesting?"

"Maybe she just took off," Quist said. "The marriage wasn't as great as you all thought. No children. She wanted out. She had money."

"And has stayed hidden for seven years? That's crazy, Mr. Quist. She couldn't stay hidden. Everybody in the world would know her by sight. She was as familiar as a TV series star, as a Joan Crawford or a Bette Davis in their primes. No way."

"While I'm being crazy let me go one step further,"

Quist said. "Changing faces was Dr. Martine's business."

He looked steadily at the blond girl behind the desk for a moment, and then he turned and walked out of the office.

3

Perhaps one of the reasons that Lieutenant Kreevich and Julian Quist got along so well is that their minds had a way of working along the same channels at the same time.

Quist left Dilys Johns in Bart's office, went out into the darkness of a late winter afternoon, street lights showing a faint sprinkling of snow which melted almost as quickly as it hit the pavement. Headed for home, Quist decided to walk a few blocks up Park Avenue. He needed to sort out his thoughts and, at the same time, get his blood circulating again. He felt physically tied up from hours of tension. Suddenly he was at Thirty-eighth Street, and Dr. Martine's house was less than a block away, eastward. Kreevich might be there. Quist thought he would like to share with his friend what Dilys had called "crazy," and to find out if it was already too late to save Bart from political disaster.

His luck was in. A policeman in the building's vestibule told him that Kreevich was, in fact, there. The lieutenant was in Dr. Martine's reception room along with Sergeant Kaminski and Ruth Taylor, the doctor's receptionist. She was trying to put scattered file folders together, restoring some sort of order to the chaos the killer had left behind.

110

Kreevich was at the receptionist's desk, studying the contents of a folder that didn't look like the others in the office. He had a kind of keyed-up frustration about him that meant the combination to the safe wasn't falling into place.

"I trust you've come to tell me you've got your man hogtied and where he belongs," Kreevich said.

"Sorry. No sign of him, no word from him."

"I've just about run out of patience with that sonofabitch, except that George Strock turned up the taxi driver."

"Bart's story checks?"

"As to time, yes. The driver, of course, doesn't know what was going on in his mind." The lieutenant slapped at the folder in front of him. "Would you believe I'm trying to solve a seven-year-old case, long closed, instead of the one that's right here in front of me? Missing Persons' complete failure to locate a trace of Maureen Craven."

"Would you believe I stopped by because Maureen was on my mind?"

Kreevich's narrowed eyes brightened. "You dug up something?"

"Just questions," Quist said.

"Hell, I can give you questions till they come out of your ears!" Kreevich said. "Go ahead, add to them."

"I find myself interested in money," Quist said. "She wasn't broke when she met Bart. She was a success. What did she do with her money?"

Kreevich turned over some pages in his folder. "A smart cop asked that question seven years ago," he said. "She made only four pictures, you know—three in England, one here. I'm talking about lead parts. She played bits and extras in half a dozen others in England. Here it is." He read from the folder. "She got roughly fifteen thousand dollars in American money for the three leads she made in England."

"Each?"

"Each. She got two hundred grand for the film she made here. A little more than a quarter of a million. A substitute outfielder makes that playing a season of baseball today! But she wasn't broke."

"What did she do? Throw it into a family kitty?"

"That smart cop seven years ago asked that question, chum. What do you think your friend Mr. Craven answered to that?"

"I'll bite."

"He never knew there was any money. He never asked her, she never mentioned it."

"That's hard to believe."

"That smart cop, seven years ago, didn't believe it either. But he was never able to find a trace of it. No bank account in England, no bank account anywhere here. Your Mr. Craven said money wasn't of any consequence; he had plenty. She never mentioned it, he never thought about it. Five years married and he never thought about a quarter of a million bucks floating around some place."

"After taxes it could have been half of that. Did she have a family, parents she might have passed it on to when she married?"

"Not a soul anywhere. That smart cop never came up with a blessed thing, Julian."

Quist was silent for a moment. "Did you ever hear of mad money, Mark?"

"Sure. Girl goes out on a date with a strange guy. She has taxi fare hidden away in case they don't get along."

"So we have a young woman of twenty-five," Quist said. "Young, but sophisticated; a rising film star, probably dozens of guys after her. Independence would

112

be important for such a girl. And she had the money stashed away to *be* independent when she met Bart Craven. Then something she doesn't believe could really happen happens. She falls wildly, totally, irresponsibly in love with an older man. She's ready to give up her career. She's willing to ride to the ends of the earth with him on a one-hump camel if he asks. She will have a half a dozen kids, a whole new world, and love, love, love. But our Maureen is a realist. She may be out of her mind; she may be under the spell of some magic love potion; she may find she is headed, not for a dream world, but for the offshore rocks. So she stashes away her mad money, just in case."

"Then five perfect years, from all accounts—except for no kids," Kreevich said.

"From all accounts," Quist said. "Those 'all accounts' coming from Jack Milburn, Bart's best friend; Rachel Hoyt, who has been Bart's mother-housekeeper for forty years; and Dilys Johns, Bart's secretary who is, incidentally, in love with him."

"And fifty other people my smart cop of seven years ago asked about the marriage," Kreevich said. "Made in heaven, that marriage, they all said. But your point is?"

"I don't know about your smart cop," Quist said, "but I haven't run across anyone who was Maureen's close friend and confidant. Rachel, and Dilys, and Jack Milburn all saw the marriage from Bart's side of the street. They were all delighted with how happy he was, how he'd blossomed. But there was at least one thing wrong with it all from Maureen's point of view. No kids. Who did she talk to about that? Were there other problems? She has a month alone while he goes to the Middle East for the State Department. She decides to end it. She has her mad money."

113

Kreevich sounded impatient. "So what? She buys an island in the South Pacific and disappears forever? She's a decent kind of woman, we're told, and she inflicts that kind of punishment on her husband? Why doesn't she just tell him it doesn't work, go back to her career, eventually find Mr. Right for herself?"

"I don't know," Quist admitted.

"And while you're playing with this invention, chum, tie Dr. Martine into it for me. He stopped over at her island for a drink of water and found her there? 'Pay up, lady, or I'll talk?' It doesn't make the slightest bit of sense, Julian."

"You're right, it doesn't," Quist said, after a moment.

"But Martine did involve himself, unless your friend is lying through his teeth," Kreevich said. "What had he found out, after seven years? Something my smart cop of the time couldn't find, something Strock hasn't found after six years of searching. I ask myself that over and over until my brains rattle."

"Somewhere there is a close friend of Maureen's in whom she confided," Quist said.

"And that close friend has kept her mouth shut for seven years while the whole damn world looked for Maureen?"

"Could be that friend believes what we really believe, Mark. It was a mugger, a sex nut. What Maureen confided won't bring her back, and would only hurt Bart."

"So what good would it do us to find her—or him?" Kreevich asked.

"Not much, I suppose."

Kreevich closed the Missing Persons folder and leaned back in his chair, looking up at Quist. "Seven years ago this smart cop"—and Kreevich slapped the folder—"didn't have one lead that we have, Julian. Dr.

Claude Martine wasn't on stage seven years ago, but night before last he claimed to know what happened then. He doesn't appear in my smart cop's investigation, but he has to belong there. For God's sake, find your friend Craven and get him to come clean with us, Julian. Meanwhile I'm going to take Dr. Claude Martine's history apart, brick by brick, till I find out where it touches Maureen Craven. Because it has to touch somewhere. It *has* to!"

Being a favored friend of the lieutenant's, Quist was given a ride home from Thirty-eighth Street to his apartment building on Beekman Place in an unmarked police car by Sergeant Kaminski. The sergeant, like Kreevich, had been on continuous duty for nearly twenty-four hours and was entitled to some sleep if he was to continue functioning. Driving Quist didn't take him very far out of his way to an uptown apartment where he lived.

"Doesn't Mark ever sleep?" Quist asked the dour-faced Sergeant.

"Not till he has something to go to bed with, something that he thinks is a handle to his case," Kaminski said.

"Where will he go to look for these 'bricks' he was talking about?"

"Back to 1973," Kaminski said. He stopped the car for a red crossing light. Light snow was falling again, the windshield wipers clicking back and forth. "The smart cop he was talking about earlier was a first-class investigator named Danforth, Sergeant Steve Danforth. He didn't have Dr. Martine to work with back then. Maybe the lieutenant will find a way to connect Martine with Maureen Craven, a connection Danforth had no reason to try to make."

115

"None of the people close to the Cravens ever heard of Dr. Martine until last night."

"They say," Kaminski said. The light turned green and he moved on uptown again. "Your man Craven is hard to figure, Mr. Quist. Is it possible he can be some place he hasn't heard the latest—the murder of Pete Gamage? There isn't a saloon, a home television set, a taxi cab radio, where the news isn't being shouted. The same killer strikes again. He has to know that. He's just sitting somewhere, licking his wounds and blowing his future—according to you and his other friends."

"You don't believe that?"

"Let me tell you how it is, Mr. Quist. I don't believe the lieutenant, or any of us in Homicide, can afford to assume it. In case he isn't innocent, in case he's a crazy man on a revenge kick of some sort, we've given him almost two days in which to play his next billing or take off for the moon, if that's where he thinks he'll be safe. In a few hours the lieutenant will send out a general alarm for him, but, in my judgment, that's way too late."

"You've told Kreevich how you feel?"

"Yes. But I don't argue with the lieutenant. Ninety-nine percent of the time his instincts about a situation turn out to be right. That's why the commissioner and most of us think he's the best. About the time everyone starts to scream that he's mishandled this, your Mr. Craven will turn up in a Turkish bath where he's been holed up in a steam room trying to forget his troubles."

"I hope," Quist said.

It was about six-thirty when Quist walked into his own apartment where Lydia was on hand to greet him. The world seemed to get back on its axis as he held her for a moment. Suppose she were gone, lost, beyond the skills of the police to find, beyond his own abilities to locate?

116

"I might bury myself, periodically, to find a reason for going on at all," he said.

Lydia leaned back from his embrace to look up at him. "What are you talking about, love?" she asked.

"If you suddenly vanished," he said.

"No news of Bart?"

"None," he said.

"I'm not going to vanish, Julian, except to make you a drink," she said.

He sat at the living room bar, sipping his Jack Daniels on the rocks, and telling Lydia about his day, his conversations with Rachel Hoyt, with Jack Milburn, with Dilys Johns, and eventually Kreevich.

"So far nothing that adds up to anything," he said.

She sat on a bar stool next to him, a cool hand resting on his.

"I've spent a lot of today getting nowhere, too," she said. "I thought I might find something that would be useful to you."

"Oh?"

"Old newspaper files at the office, going back to 1973," she said.

"The original case?"

"Yes. Maureen's disappearance. There was a lot about her, Julian, that I hadn't remembered."

"Like?"

"You wondered if she might have given the money she had to family. There was no family. Everything about her life was a drama, Julian. Left on the steps of a Catholic convent in London, two or three days old. No mother ever surfaced, no parents of any sort. She had no name. She was delivered on St. Patrick's day, so the nuns called her Patricia. Would you believe 'Patricia Blank'?"

"Oh, brother!"

"For seventeen years the nuns raised her, educated her. Did a pretty marvelous job from all accounts. When she was seventeen the nuns put on some kind of pageant, in which Patricia Blank played a leading role. In the audience was a well-known British actress, top flight, named Nadine Connors. Miss Connors was fascinated by Patricia Blank. She suggested that there was a part the girl could play in a film she was about to make. The nuns agreed, the girl, of course, was eager. She played a bit in Miss Connors's film, using a name she made up, I guess—Maureen Tate. It was the beginning of a career that grew into something big. Three years of small parts, then featured, then starred. Nadine Connors was her sponsor, her friend, her acting inspiration. Top of the heap, Maureen comes to America to make a film in Hollywood, big salary, on the way to whatever she wanted. She meets Bart, fifteen years older, and gives up everything for love, marriage, hopefully kids."

"That explains, perhaps, why she went for an older man," Quist said. "Never had a father. Bart wasn't old enough to be her father, but he was a sort of father figure."

"Maybe. But that isn't what interested me," Lydia said. "If there is anyone in the world with whom Maureen might have discussed private problems, private difficulties, it would be the woman who launched her on her career, Nadine Connors."

"She never came forward with anything, did she?"

"No. She was interviewed at the time, had nothing but glowing comments to make about Maureen as an actress, as a person. Nothing that suggested she knew anything about any problems that would account for a disappearance."

"So that's that," Quist said.

"Maybe," Lydia said. "How would you like to go to the theater, Julian?"

"Tonight? Oh, look, sweet, I . . ."

"You don't follow the theater the way I do, love," Lydia said. "There's a British comedy, all British cast, playing at the Stetson Theater. In the character lead, with first-class notices from Walter Kerr, Doug Watt, and others, is Miss Nadine Connors."

Quist glanced at his watch. "We should just be able to make the first act curtain," he said.

British comedy, high style, has a certain patina, a certain sheen, that even a Neil Simon or a Woody Allen doesn't possess. And Miss Nadine Connors was, Quist thought, a past master at the art of comedic playing. Or should he say "past mistress"? She had to be in her late seventies, yet she still moved with a kind of fluid grace and elegance. Her voice was like a deep bell, each note clear and unmarred by time. Her timing, the slipping of innuendo into an apparently innocent line by a gesture, the movement of an eyebrow, the widening of huge dark eyes into an expression of innocence that you weren't meant to believe for an instant—she had control of all the techniques and she delighted her audience with them. Miss Connors was so very good, as was the rest of the company, that Quist was almost able to stop thinking about the last forty-eight hours. He regretted having to leave just as the applause was beginning at the end of the third act. He would have added to the volume of sound, but he wanted to get backstage with Lydia before Miss Connors had a chance to slip away.

He needn't have worried. A dozen people were crowded outside the great lady's dressing room, their voices raised in a chorus of delight and praise. Quist had taken a business card from his wallet and written on it:

"*I was a friend of Maureen Tate's. May we please talk?*" He slipped it to a maid who was holding off the visitors until Miss Connors "gets out of her costume." When people were finally admitted, the maid stopped Quist and Lydia.

"Would you mind very much waiting till the others go, sir? Miss Connors would prefer to talk to you alone."

They could, of course, wait. From the half-open dressing door came a collection of "*dah*lings" and "*mah*velouses" and squeals of pleasure. Miss Connors's booming voice carried over it all. She was regretting having to cut the visit short: "Do come back another time, but I have business I *must* discuss with . . ."—in a stage whisper—"*a Hollywood producer!*"

After a moment or two the visitors began to exit. They all eyed Quist curiously. He looked, they thought, the way a Hollywood tycoon should look—handsome, perfectly dressed, with a beautiful woman holding his arm.

The maid was at the door, beckoning to them. There was nothing starlike about Miss Connors's dressing room. It was a long, narrow room, with a makeup mirror lighted by colored bulbs backing up a makeup table. There was a rack for costumes Miss Connors wore in the play and another for her own clothes. There was a thick rug covering a cement floor, three or four straight-backed chairs, a cot on which the great lady probably rested on matinee days, a sort of highboy-bureau. It was obvious Miss Connors didn't hold court in the place where she worked.

When Quist and Lydia came in Miss Connors was sitting at the mirror, wearing a smocklike dressing gown. The bright, scarlet hair Quist had admired on stage was resting on a wig stand. Miss Connors's own

120

hair was white, clipped very short—probably since she had to wear the wig eight times a week. She turned from the mirror and her face was smeared with a cream for removing makeup. It was almost as if she deliberately meant to be unrecognizable. She wasn't the woman they'd seen on stage or the one they'd be likely to meet on the street. The voice, however, was not to be confused with one belonging to anyone else.

"You should be more careful, Mr. Quist, about what you say in public and what you write on your business card," she said.

"Oh?"

"I read an interview with you in the afternoon paper. You are promoting Bart Craven's political career. You said in that interview that you had never met Maureen, so you were, obviously, never a friend of hers."

"I apologize, Miss Connors. After the last two days I feel as if I'd known her very well. This is Miss Morton. She is one of the 'associates' mentioned on my business card."

"How lucky for you," Miss Connors said. The reading of the line had a kind of perfection.

"Miss Connors, it would take me a long time, longer then either of us has, for me to go over this case with you, step by step," Quist said. "I am Bart Craven's friend. I'm also connected with him professionally. The Homicide detective in charge of the case, Lieutenant Kreevich, is also a close, personal friend. It's fair to say that I am involved."

"I've read whatever has been in the papers," Miss Connors said, "and listened to the telly in my hotel room when I could. Shocking business."

"We haven't been able to make a connection, Miss Connors, between Maureen Craven and Dr. Claude

Martine, who was murdered night before last. As you know, he called Bart Craven to tell him he knew what had happened to Maureen. When Bart got there to hear whatever this doctor had to tell, he found the doctor and his nurse shot to death."

There was no readable expression on the grease-covered face of the actress. "Why have you come to me?" she asked.

"Because you were so very close to Maureen. You spotted her in a convent pageant, you got her into films. She must have confided in you, talked to you. You're the first close friend of hers I've been able to identify who isn't a friend of her husband's."

"Is that so odd?" Miss Connors asked. "She was British. She married an American and settled here in New York. Except for new friends she may have made during the six months she was in Hollywood, any friends she had in this country she must have met through her husband, through the life they lived here in New York. I—I was close to her long ago. You know her beginnings? No family, just the nuns who brought her up, educated her."

"You found her and brought her out into the real world."

"Yes, I suppose you could say that. And, yes, it was all so new, so exciting, so different, and I was the one person in that new world she could come to for advice, for explanations."

"And that friendship lasted?"

"Yes—if you take into account that we were most of the time on opposite sides of an ocean, she here, I in London."

"But you stayed in touch. You met Bart, of course?"

"Would you believe that I never did—while she was

122

still here? Five years. I had plays and films in England, she had her marriage here in the States. We wrote occasionally, though neither of us were very great letter writers. We got in touch by phone, maybe once–twice a year. Just girl chatter."

"She talked about her marriage, how it was going?"

"Dream come true, and things like that. The first and only times I saw her, after her marriage, was in the last month she was alive. I stopped in New York on the way to Hollywood where I was to do a film. We saw each other every day for about a week. I didn't meet her husband because he was in the Middle East on a job for the government."

"So you and she had time to catch up on each other," Quist said.

Miss Connors's laugh came from deep down in her chest somewhere. "Chatter, chatter, chatter," she said.

"How had the marriage worn by then?" Quist asked.

The old actress turned to the makeup mirror and began to remove cream from her face with cleansing tissues. She stared at herself, as though she were answering the person in the mirror, not Quist.

"How do most marriages go after five years?" she asked. "Wears a little thin here, roots grow deeper there. No relationship stays the same forever, Mr. Quist. If it did, we would all die of boredom."

"Where had Maureen's marriage worn thin?"

The old actress brought her fist down on the table, and the jars of cosmetics bounced around. "Maureen's private life is hers to keep to herself, even in the grave," she said. She drew a deep breath. "She was disappointed that there'd been no children. She wanted them very much. The family doctor had assured her that there was no basic reason they shouldn't have them, sooner or later. Aside from that, everything was splendid."

"Did she talk to you about the possibility of going back to acting?"

"Yes. I think her husband urged her to. He told me he had when I talked to him."

"I thought you said you'd never met him."

"I told you I'd never met him while Maureen was alive. He came to England, after she'd gone, looking for something that would help find her. It was all quite futile, of course. If Maureen were alive, Mr. Quist, he'd have known where she was. She would never, never, *never* have walked out on him and left him flat, without an explanation."

"You say things change, Miss Connors," Lydia said, speaking for the first time. "Was it that Bart was no longer a great lover, but had become a great friend?"

Nadine Connors's smile at Quist was reflected in the mirror. "Look out for that girl, Quist. She may be too smart for you." She turned around in her chair to face them directly. "You two have almost made me break a rule. I would never repeat any gossip that would hurt another human being. If gossip about her marriage would bring Maureen back, or explain her disappearance, perhaps I would gossip. She is dead, Mr. Quist. All I can do is assure you that there was nothing wrong that had Maureen thinking about an end to her marriage. She was deeply in love with her husband, no matter what the intimate details of their life together may have been. Is there anything else?" She sounded, suddenly, very tired.

"Money," Quist said. "She was very well-off when she met Bart. She'd had a big salary in Hollywood. Did she ever tell you what she'd done with her money?"

Miss Connors seemed to have lost interest. "No. I

124

mean, her husband must have involved himself in her finances. Have you asked him?"

"I will—when I can," Quist said. "One more thing, Miss Connors. Dr. Martine? Did Maureen ever mention him to you."

"I never heard of him till I read the papers yesterday," Miss Connors said.

"Do you know if Maureen ever got involved with some kind of cosmetic surgery? Actresses in films do, you know."

That deep-chested laugh surfaced again. "My God, Mr. Quist, she was a gem of beauty. She was perfect. There would have been no possible way to improve on her looks."

There seemed to be no further place to go. Quist and Lydia left Nadine Connors staring at her own reflection in the makeup mirror. They flagged a cab outside the theater and headed for home.

"You seem to have rung some kind of bell with the old girl," Quist said. "Your great-lover, great-friend routine."

Lydia rested her dark head against his shoulder for an instant, laughing softly. "Don't let it worry you, love," she said. "You're a far better lover today then you were the first time you tried your talents on me."

"Flattery will get you anything and everything," Quist said. He bent down and touched her forehead with his lips. "I enjoyed the play, but Miss Connors didn't produce very much for us."

"Perhaps if we let it marinate until morning we'll find something there we missed," Lydia said.

The telephone was ringing as they let themselves into the apartment. Quist crossed to the bar and picked up the extension there.

"Mr. Quist? I've been trying to reach you for quite a while." It was Sergeant Kaminski's flat, emotionless voice.

"You haven't had much sleep, Sergeant," Quist said.

"I thought you'd better know before it came at you from the tube or the radio," Kaminski said. "Kreevich got it."

"You mean the tie-in between Maureen and Dr. Martine?"

"I mean he got it!" Kaminski said. He sounded savage. "He was shot, just outside St. Margaret's Hospital, about an hour ago."

"How bad is it?" Quist asked, shaky.

"Bad. He's in emergency at St. Margaret's. Four or five shots in the chest and neck. They—they don't think he's going to make it, Mr. Quist."

"Who did it? Did he say?"

"He hasn't been able to speak a word. He's out, gone—goddamn it!"

PART THREE

1

Not possible to take in! Not believable! Kreevich!

St. Margaret's Hospital had turned into a minor madhouse. Quist thought he had never seen so many policemen in one place, short of a parade. There was a huge corps of reporters, many of whom Quist knew. In the crowded lobby of the hospital he caught up with Rusty Grimes, the *Newsview* man.

"Your friend, isn't he?" Rusty asked.

Quist nodded.

"Good man. It shouldn't have happened to him."

"What did happen, Rusty? I've been out of touch all evening. On the phone Sergeant Kaminski just told me Mark had been shot, was on the critical list."

Grimes' rumpled his bright red hair. "He apparently came here to go over records that covered the activities of Dr. Claude Martine. They gave him some office space and files. He spent a couple of hours, then walked out the front entrance about nine-thirty. Someone was waiting for him. Must have been almost face to face with him, shots were fired that close up. No way the killer could miss."

"He's not a killer yet."

"Isn't he?" Grimes was angry. "Three people yesterday, the lieutenant tonight."

Quist hung onto his own rage. "Are you telling me Mark has gone, Rusty?"

"Not yet—I think," Grimes said. "It's a minute-to-minute thing, according to Captain Larsen."

"Who is Captain Larsen?"

"Chief of Homicide, in charge."

"Where is he?"

Grimes shrugged. "They've set up an office, but I think he's in the operating room."

"Any kind of witness?"

"No. Nobody's come forward who heard anything. A nurse, coming on duty, found the lieutenant in an ocean of blood on the front steps."

A hand closed on Quist's arm. It was Sergeant Kaminski. His face was the color of dirty parchment.

"You got here," he said.

"Fast as I could."

"Captain Larsen wants to talk to you. This way."

They wedged their way through the crowd of cops and reporters to a corridor which led to a small reception room, bright from fluorescent ceiling lights, bare, cold. There was a table, three or four straight chairs. This is where they tell you your friend had just died on the operating table, Quist thought. It was now set aside for the police.

"The captain's in the operating theater," Kaminski said. "He knows you're one of the lieutenant's close friends. Also that you have a connection, in a way, with the case he was working on." He turned away, a nerve twitching at the corner of his mouth. "I shouldn't have left him. I should never have left him! I guess he came here to look for those 'bricks' he was talking about." He

130

turned back to Quist and his eyes were frozen. "Where is your friend Craven? *Now* we put out an alarm for him. I told you it was too damn late!"

Waiting was torture. There was nothing on earth for these two men to talk about except Kreevich and Kreevich's case. Each had his own private, and probably very different, feelings about the wounded man. Respect was the key to what they both felt, but a different kind of respect. Quist thought of his friend as an unusually well-rounded human being, a man with a profound understanding of human complexities, with compassion for the tensions that could drive someone up the wall, and finally, a man who was expert at his profession.

Kaminski thought of Kreevich first and last as a good cop, a man who knew more than Kaminski himself could ever hope to learn about the science of fighting crime, a man who would never ask anyone under him to face danger ahead of him. You would lay it on the line for that kind of superior officer.

"And I had to get sleep," Kaminski said, in a flat, bitter voice. "I left him alone when we both knew there was some kind of psycho running loose. Ten to one your friend Craven is floating around pumping lead into anyone who gets close to him." He spoke as though he thought Quist was to blame.

"The odds aren't quite that long, Sergeant," a voice said from behind them. A big, blond man had come through the door from the corridor. "Mr. Quist? I'm Captain Larsen." He looked like a powerful linebacker on a pro football team, all muscle, with quick blue eyes that suggested he was ready for an attack from anywhere.

"How is he, Captain?" Kaminski asked.

"Alive is about all I can tell you," Larsen said.

131

"Able to talk?" Quist asked.

"Not now, maybe never. The odds on that aren't good, Mr. Quist. The odds on Craven aren't as hot as you make them, Sergeant. We've got a fingerprint report from the Air Force that Kreevich asked for. Craven isn't the man who searched Martine's apartment, which means he didn't kill the caretaker. Which probably means he didn't kill anybody."

Quist knew he should feel relieved, but he didn't feel anything but the burning need to get revenge for his friend.

"Kreevich is still on the operating table," Larsen said. "They think another hour or two. One of the slugs is lodged in his spine. Very delicate business. Get clumsy and he might never walk or move again—if he survives. They've removed four of the six slugs that were fired into him. The man was so close there were actually powder burns on Kreevich's clothes!"

"Same gun as in the other cases?" Quist asked.

"A guess," Larsen said. "Same caliber gun. Ballistics will have to examine the rifling marks under a microscope before they say yes. But the guess is yes."

"Mark must have seen who it was."

"The gunman was a hell of a lot closer to Mark than I am to you, Mr. Quist. The entrance way is lighted. Mark saw him, for a second or two at least, before the first shot was fired."

"Bastard!" Kaminski muttered.

"I count on you to help catch me up, Mr. Quist," Larsen said. "Kaminski tells me Mark was here to check out on the disappearance of Maureen Craven. That's a seven-year-old case."

"He was trying to put Maureen Craven and Dr. Martine in the same ball park," Quist said. "Martine interned here, was on the staff here, had his hospital affiliation here when he went private. I think Mark was trying to place Maureen here in 1973, or even before that. There's nothing to indicate she'd been involved in his private practice."

Larsen nodded. "He came here about seven-thirty."

"About an hour after we left him," Kaminski said.

"Dr. Powell, the head man here at St. Margaret's, set him up in his own office with a stack of records," Larsen said. "He spent a couple of hours with those records, walked out at about nine-thirty, and got it, head on."

"What did he find?" Kaminski asked.

"No way of knowing. The stuff he went through is still in Powell's office."

"He must have made notes," Kaminski said.

"If he did they weren't anywhere on him," Larsen said.

"Sonofabitch searched him after he shot him!" Kaminski said.

"Maybe not," Larsen said. "If he found something, Mark wouldn't necessarily write it down. He may have been on his way to follow up on whatever. Or he didn't find any kind of a lead. We're going to have to go through all that material again."

"I'd like to be the one. I know the way he was thinking," Kaminski said.

"Dr. Powell's office is on the second floor," Larsen said. "Go ahead, Kaminski. There's a detective up there now, trying to sort things out."

Kaminski took off, almost running.

"Better for him to be up there than going around in circles down here," Larsen said. "He's worked with Kreevich for quite a few years. It's hard to think straight when it's someone you admire, you might even say love."

"You're telling me?" Quist said.

133

"You and Mark are close?"

"Long time. I left him a little before six. Kaminski drove me home to Beekman Place from Dr. Martine's house. We were both interested in trying to tie Martine into the Maureen Craven thing in 1973. The last thing Kreevich had said to me was that he was going to take the Maureen Craven case apart 'brick by brick' till he found out where it touched Dr. Martine."

"And you have an interest in that, too, don't you?" Larsen was unhurried, a quiet, thorough man who gave Quist a feeling of confidence.

"Yes. Bart Craven is a client of mine—and a friend. The fingerprint evidence is conclusive? Not his?"

"He didn't search the house," Larsen said. "We have dozens of prints of the man who did, so far unidentified. We don't have them in our files. The FBI in Washington doesn't have them."

Quist explained, as briefly as he could, about Bart's periods of isolation to deal with his private pain.

"Kaminski tells me that Craven talked to Kreevich about finding the killer himself," Larsen said.

"Just the wild talk of a desperate man," Quist said. "He thought the killer must have known what Martine was about to reveal. He wants to believe that there's someone alive who knows the answer."

"You don't believe that?"

"I didn't, until tonight," Quist said. A muscle rippled along the line of his jaw. "Mark wasn't shot just for the hell of it, Captain. He came here to look for that answer. The killer must have thought Mark had found it, or would find it—here at St. Margaret's."

"If he found it, we'll find it," Larsen said. "I know you want to stay here, Mr. Quist, to wait for results. It may be hours, even days. You could be more useful devoting your time to trying to find Craven, staying in constant touch with his people: the housekeeper, the secretary, the friend he may contact. Craven may have come across something, or think he has. Call me here at the hospital, anytime you want. I'll leave orders for you to be put through to me. I'll let you know exactly how things are going with Mark, anytime you call."

The night moved on into early morning, the third day of Bart Craven's silent absence. In phone conversations with Rachel Hoyt, Dilys Johns, and Jack Milburn, Quist sensed a growing hysteria among Bart's close people. Milburn put it into words.

"The shooting of Lieutenant Kreevich suggests some kind of psycho, cruising around killing anyone he thinks may know something," Milburn said. "That could include Bart, who doesn't know anything. It could include one of us. It could include you, Julian."

Hard to believe, but possible, Quist thought. It could also include George Strock, the detective, who had spent six years looking for "bricks." He called Strock and found him at home.

"I can't believe the news about the lieutenant," Strock said. "How is he doing?"

"He's still on the operating table," Quist said. "They're not too hopeful."

"God save us," Strock said. "Was he able to describe the man who shot him?"

"He hasn't been able to say anything, may never be able to. Look, George, sleep isn't going to be possible for me. I'm going to my place and stay by the phone there. There's an outside chance I might hear from Craven."

"He's still missing?"

"Yes. I thought if we spent some time exchanging ideas we might come up with something. It would be better than walking the floor. Would you be willing?"

"Of course," Strock said. "But unless there's more than I've been able to find in six years I'm not optimistic."

"Well, we can at least have a drink or two together," Quist said. "I should be home in about fifteen minutes."

"See you," Strock said.

Quist had made his calls from a public phone in the hospital lobby. He buttoned up his topcoat and walked out the main entrance. This was the way Kreevich had gone. A section of the front steps was roped off, and three cops were standing guard. There were chalk marks in the shape of a body on the steps. Kreevich had only taken two of the six steps down from the main doors when he was confronted and shot. He couldn't have dreamed it was coming.

A taxi took Quist to Beekman Place. No place in the world felt quite safe just then. He checked the street outside his apartment building before he got out of the cab. It appeared to be deserted. The killer had struck four people, all of them at close range. He didn't take sharpshooter chances.

Lydia was very much awake and waiting for him this time. He told her what news there was, and that George Strock was about to put in an appearance. He went to the phone on the bar and called the hospital. He asked for Captain Larsen, and when he gave his name he was put straight through. Larsen was a man of his word.

"He's still on the table," the captain said. "Our friend is a pretty tough fighter, Mr. Quist."

"The news is better, then?"

"He ought to be dead. He isn't," Larsen said.

"You're looking at the material he had there?"

"It's a mile high," Larsen said. "He may have known what he was looking for. We don't. So far, nothing."

136

"And nothing on Craven," Quist said. "I'm at my apartment. If anything happens with Mark before I call you again, will you let me know?"

"A promise," Larsen said.

Lydia had a bourbon on the rocks for him when Quist put down the phone.

"The political boys have been calling you every ten minutes," she said. "Tom Molloy, Paul Graves, Senator Metzger."

"The ship is sinking," Quist said. "The rats are leaving."

"Does it really matter?" Lydia asked. "Bart isn't going to run for the Senate after all this, even if they handed it to him on a platter."

"I suppose not. Mark never had a chance, you know."

"I'm sorry, love. So very sorry."

He didn't tell her what Milburn was thinking. At least here, in these rooms, they were safe. The house phone rang. The lobby man downstairs announced George Strock.

Quist took the little detective's coat and hat and introduced him to Lydia. Strock would, when asked, have a small Scotch with a dash of soda.

"It's hard to believe that a man of Kreevich's experience could have been caught off guard," he said. He settled on one of the bar stools.

"He opened the front door of the hospital, took two steps, and that was that," Quist said. "I just talked to Captain Larsen. He's still in surgery, still fighting."

"I wish I thought we could get somewhere," Strock said, and thanked Lydia for the drink she brought him. "Craven, I suppose, is the cops' chief suspect?"

"Maybe not, although they're naturally wondering about him," Quist said. "Your taxi driver helped. Now they know he wasn't the man who searched Dr. Martine's house and, presumably, shot the caretaker. Finger prints don't match."

"Good," Strock said. "The poor bastard's had enough bad luck for one lifetime. What was Kreevich after at the hospital, do you know?"

"Some connection between Maureen Craven and Dr. Martine," Quist said.

Strock shook his head slowly. "Nothing, in six years of searching."

"But you weren't looking for that connection," Quist said. "I assume you never heard of Dr. Martine until he was killed, night before last."

Strock eyes were narrowed behind the wire-rimmed glasses. "In a way true, but in a way not true," he said.

"Meaning?"

"I'd heard of him, but not in any way that's connected with Maureen Craven." Strock sipped his drink. "In my business, looking for missing people, when there's a disaster somewhere you check. A plane crash, a bombing, a fire. St. Margaret's has a famous burn unit. I've had occasion to go there several times in the past years. I knew that Dr. Martine was their top man for burn surgery. I never met him. As a matter of fact I never found anyone I was looking for at St. Margaret's so I never got into the setup there very deeply. I knew, from talking to Kreevich yesterday, that he was wondering if Maureen had ever had any cosmetic surgery. First time the doctor's name ever came up in the same conversation."

"You told him she hadn't?"

"You know, Mr. Quist," Strock said, shifting his weight on the bar stool, "I have made what you might call a life study of Maureen Craven. I can tell you, without any fear of contradiction, that she never had

138

any cosmetic surgery, not even the most minor kind, like the removal of a mole. I can tell you that she had extraordinarily good teeth, only three small fillings at age thirty. I can tell you that she hadn't varied a pound in weight in ten years, and that she didn't have to diet or embark on any kind of exercise program to hold it where she wanted it. Her menstrual periods were regular and without complications."

"That is really intimate information," Lydia said.

"I didn't mean to be vulgar, Miss Morton," Strock said. "I just want to make it clear that I made a study of this woman I was searching for: dental charts, medical reports. I can tell you that her classic measurements were thirty-six, twenty-two, thirty-two. I can tell you the size shoe she wore, who designed her clothes, I can give you an itemized list of her jewelry, insured and uninsured."

"Her bank account?" Quist asked.

"She had a joint checking account with Craven. Used it to supply herself with small amounts of cash, shopping money."

"She had over a quarter of a million in earnings, before taxes, when she married Bart," Quist said. "Where is it?"

Strock glanced at Lydia. "Do you mind if I smoke, Miss Morton?" he asked.

"Of course not."

He took a small flat box of dark cigarillos from his pocket and lit one with a Zippo lighter. "I didn't come on the case, Mr. Quist, until ten months after Maureen disappeared. September third, 1973, was the day she was gone. Bart Craven didn't hire me until June of 1974. Up till then Missing Persons had had the case. Sergeant Danforth, a good man, let me see all the records. That question had come up. Where was her money? Danforth wondered if she'd just taken off, run out on the marriage, with plenty of bread to finance herself. He never found any trace of a bank account. Bart Craven drew a blank on it. Maureen, he said, had never mentioned money of hers to him. He hadn't cared, he didn't need it, it didn't matter to him."

"And you took Danforth's word for it that there was no bank account anywhere?"

"The hell I did," Strock said. "When I take a case I don't take anyone's word for anything. The best investigator in the world can miss the boat somewhere. I dig out my own answers."

"And?"

"I checked all over the city here. No bank account. I checked in England, I checked in Hollywood. Nothing. She grew up with nothing, she suddenly had quite a bit. She spent money very freely, I found. She bought furs, jewelry, couple of expensive cars, all before she married Bart. She was in Hollywood for six or eight months when she first came to this country to make a film. She rented what might be called a mansion out there. She had a personal maid, a couple of house servants. She dined and partied at the most expensive places. I gathered she was more than generous with almost casual acquaintances who needed financial help. After taxes she probably didn't have anything like a quarter of a million. I decided she'd just spent it as she went along. She was only twenty-five when she met Bart Craven. She had a hot future ahead of her. She hadn't needed to be cautious with money. She wanted luxury after a pretty grim growing up. She gave up her career, her future, when she married Bart, but that didn't matter because he is loaded."

"That explains the money, I guess," Quist said.

"I think it does," Strock said. "It was the only thing I

could come up with. There had been a small bank account in England, just used for day-to-day stuff, you understand. It was closed out when she went to Hollywood. She drew a few hundred pounds, all that was left. She opened an account in Hollywood. A lot of money passed through it. But when she'd finished her film she closed that out, only a few thousand bucks left. Then she was married to Bart for five years, spent money like water on clothes, trinkets, parties, theaters—and presents for him. Gold cuff links, black pearl studs, a lot of little things. I suspect she used her own money for those gifts, and that's where it went."

The phone on the end of the bar rang. It was Captain Larsen.

"He's off the table and in intensive care," Larsen told Quist.

"They think?"

"Touch and go," Larsen said. "Not too bright a picture. Anything on Craven?"

"Not yet. Have you come up with anything on the material Mark was going through at the hospital?"

"According to Dr. Powell, the administrator here, Kreevich was looking for any kind of disaster that might have taken place about the time Maureen disappeared, something that might have brought her as a patient into the burn unit where Dr. Martine was in charge."

"You found anything?"

"Yes and no," Larsen said. "The night of the day Mrs. Craven disappeared there was a fire in a fleabag hotel on Broadway. Place called the Fairmount. By coincidence, the Fairmount was only about three blocks from the Cravens' apartment on Gramercy Park. The fire destroyed the building, particularly the upper floors. About a dozen badly burned people were brought to St. Margaret's. Martine was in charge. But no Mrs. Craven,

Quist. Danforth checked and double-checked seven years ago. Everyone who was treated checked out, tied to their proper backgrounds. Four people died, one unidentified woman."

"So one person didn't check out," Quist said. He felt his muscles tightening.

"But that dead woman wasn't Maureen Craven," Larsen said. "Danforth had dental charts, other specifications on Mrs. Craven. They didn't match with the dead woman's. She wasn't Mrs. Craven. It's a coincidence that Mrs. Craven disappeared and there was the Fairmount fire, both on September third. But no connection. Everyone accounted for except a woman who wasn't Mrs. Craven."

"Nothing else?"

"Not so far. We're digging."

"Kreevich must have found something, or the killer must have thought he would find something."

"I know."

"Well, thanks for calling," Quist said. He put down the phone and turned to Strock. "Larsen has been telling me about a fire at the Fairmount Hotel. Mean anything to you, George?"

Strock put down his empty glass on the bar and Lydia took it for a refill. "My dear Mr. Quist," the little detective said. "How can I convince you that I'm really good at what I do? When I came on the case, ten months after it began, I saw the Fairmount fire as a hot lead. Danforth had written it off, but I started right at the beginning again. There had been an unidentified dead woman."

"Larsen told me."

"Danforth had headed straight for her, like the good bird dog he was. You look for what's right there, close by. Danforth was only three, four days off the pace, you understand. Missing Persons wasn't called in for that long. Craven came home from his mission to Europe early, two days early. He was disappointed not to find his wife, but he didn't press the panic button until she didn't show up on the day he'd been expected."

"He didn't panic, even though Mrs. Hoyt hadn't been told by Maureen that she wouldn't be home for a couple of nights?" Quist asked.

"I wouldn't say he didn't sweat a little," Strock said. "But Maureen wasn't obligated to be there. Beautiful warm summer day, that September third. Windows, doors to the apartment terrace open. Maureen could have left a note that—that blew out of sight somewhere. Rachel Hoyt was more upset than Bart, I think. She'd spoken with Maureen just before Maureen went out that day. Nothing was said about her not coming back. Mrs. Hoyt asked her about dinner. Maureen told her she had no plans, but she might dine out somewhere with someone, nothing definite. If she decided to come home, she'd 'picnic.' It was out of character for her not to tell Mrs. Hoyt if she wasn't coming home at all, or for her not to call if she made plans on the spur of the moment. She was a thoughtful person. Of course, she had no idea Bart was coming home that day. But to get back to Danforth. You can find his report at Missing Persons, you know."

"So could Kreevich," Quist said. "You tell me."

"The Fairmount fire was there, same day, same evening," Strock said. "Same neighborhood, you might say. But let me tell you something about the place. It may have been a nice residence hotel when it was built in 1890, but it was a pretty seedy joint on September third, 1973; a few welfare cases lived there, a lot of cheap rooms available for transients who didn't have to have luggage." Strock glanced at Lydia. "A place where call girls could take out-of-town johns and no questions asked. There were no attractions for the casual passer-by. There was a bar, patronized mostly by neighborhood bums. It was the last place in the world where an elegant lady like Maureen Craven would go. She wouldn't stop in there for a drink with someone. There were a dozen places within a stone's throw from the Fairmount that would have been infinitely better for anything casual. Danforth asked himself if it could have been an emergency." Strock glanced at Lydia again. "Maybe she had to go to the bathroom real bad and was trapped in the ladies room by the fire. Except there was no fire to speak of on the ground floor. It was the upper stories, the bedroom floors, that were gutted. Anyway —there were thirteen people in that holocaust taken to St. Margaret's burn unit." Strock reached into the inside pocket of his suit coat and brought out a worn-looking notebook. "I brought this with me. It lists most of the things I've checked out in six years." He turned to an early page. "I'm right, thirteen burn victims. Four of them died. All of them identified and accounted for by Danforth except one dead woman, who wasn't Maureen. Teeth chart didn't match, measurements didn't match. Danforth saw the body in the morgue. He described her as a flat-chested old biddy about forty-five or fifty years old."

"That would seem to be that," Quist said.

The corner of Strock's mouth twitched. "I've seen a lot of people who died violently in my time," he said. "I've seen people who've been shot, people who hanged themselves, people smashed up in car accidents, run over by a subway train, killed in plane crashes, people drowned. The worst, I think, the hardest to look at, are people who have been badly burned. The pain is so great. Faces that look like charred blankets with holes in

144

them. Would you believe I eventually saw some of those people who'd been in the Fairmount fire. Martine may have been a genius, but there were some pretty ghastly faces to look at; not easy to stomach. I satisfied myself that everyone was accounted for except the one dead woman. The other three who died had been identified by their families, decently buried."

"So what else could Kreevich have found in the files at St. Margaret's?" Quist asked.

"I can't begin to guess," Strock said. "Danforth has covered it all, I've covered it all. We each came at it from our own direction. Kreevich went at it from his. I think he would have wound up where Danforth and I did—dead end."

"The killer didn't think so."

Strock shrugged. "The killer is hyped up, gone psycho," he said.

"One more thing about the Fairmount," Quist said. It was a dead end, long ago proved out, and yet he couldn't drop it. Kreevich had been on it, and Kreevich was fighting for his life. "That unidentified dead woman, no inquiries that led to her? No questions asked by Missing Persons bureaus somewhere else?"

"No," Strock said. "Danforth covered everything and I double checked his coverage. It's routine for Missing Persons from other cities to ask questions when there's been a disaster somewhere else. No one was asking for anyone who could have been that dame."

"No identification, no handbag, no clothes labels?"

Strock shook his head. "You'll find in other records that the Fire Department believed the Fairmount was a case of arson. Maybe the owners wanted to collect insurance, though it was never proved. But the upper floors of the Fairmount were an inferno when the fire companies got there. The people who were dragged to

St. Margaret's weren't much more than burned meat. No possessions, no clothes, no nothing." The detective reached for his fresh drink and sipped it. He gave Lydia a shy little smile. "Just exactly right, Miss Morton," he said.

"Best bartender on the East Side," Quist said. He wasn't really there. His mind kept playing with an invented picture, like a movie film that was run for a few frames, rewound, and run over again. The picture showed Mark Kreevich, tying a blue and white polka-dot scarf, Ascot fashion, around his neck and slipping into his brown tweed topcoat with the zipped-in lining. He thanked someone who wasn't visible on Quist's "film," put on his hat and gave the brim a tug downward, and walked down the corridor to the front doors. Quist imagined he could hear the hollow click of Mark's heels on the marble floor. Mark opens the door and steps out. There a giant of a man faces him, coat collar turned up, hat pulled forward so that his face is hidden. He is holding a gun, right at Mark's chest. Kreevich makes a quick, desperate move, but too late. He is already going down as the killer fires the second shot at him. The killer empties his gun at Kreevich, six shots, and then disappears into the night, running down what appears to be an endless flight of stairs into a dark nowhere.

"You trying to visualize it?" Strock asked. He had lit the second of his little cigarillos.

"Trying to make sense out of nothing," Quist said. "I can't believe that the man who shot Mark gave him even a moment to be aware of what was coming. Mark is too quick, too well trained. This guy was waiting for him just outside the front door and took him, without questions, without hesitating one second. He had to know Mark was in the hospital and would be coming

146

out; he had to be certain that Mark would have found something incriminating in the records at St. Margaret's."

"Or couldn't run the risk that he hadn't," Strock said.

"Somewhere, somewhere, somewhere there has to be something that will connect Martine with Maureen Craven," Quist said. "Where do we look, Strock? That's your kind of business."

"At St. Margaret's, back in Martine's house," Strock said.

"The killer spent hours going over Martine's house, his files."

"And was interrupted by the caretaker," Strock said.

"So I'm guessing he didn't find what he was looking for," Quist said. "How does the scenario read then? If it wasn't in Martine's house—what the killer was looking for—then what?"

Strock flicked the ash from his cigarillo into a brass ash tray on the bar. "Kreevich, a very smart cop, is the enemy," he said. "The killer keeps him under surveillance. When Kreevich finally goes to St. Margaret's, the killer knows he can come up with the answer there. So he waits for him to come out, shoots him."

"But if Mark found something, he wouldn't have kept it a secret! He was working in Dr. Powell's office, right by telephones. He would have reported to headquarters, called Captain Larsen, his immediate superior. If he could have named somebody, he would have named him."

Strock took off his glasses and cleaned them with his handkerchief, blowing on the lenses first to fog them. "A very thorough man, the lieutenant," he said. "Let's say he found something in the files at St. Margaret's, but it's not quite conclusive. He needs something else to make it hang together before he reports. The killer

147

knows that's how it will be and he stops the lieutenant in his tracks." Strock put his glasses back on, carefully. "We're wasting time with guesses, Mr. Quist. Do you suppose Captain Larsen would let me go through those St. Margaret files?" He patted his little notebook. "With six years worth of information I've collected on Maureen Craven perhaps I can match up something with something."

"I'm sure he will," Quist said. "Does it occur to you, George, that this crazy killer may be watching and guess why you're going to St. Margaret's?"

Strock indulged in a thin smile. He patted a little bulge under his left armpit. "I've been watching for ambushes all my career, Mr. Quist. I'm not likely to be caught flat-footed the way the lieutenant was."

2

Policemen do not like cop-killers. Long hours after Lieutenant Kreevich had been shot down on the steps of St. Margaret's, cops were still patiently covering the neighborhood, going to every house that had a window overlooking the hospital. The shooting had taken place at night, but the hospital entrance was covered by floodlights. An action happening there would have been almost more noticeable than it would be in broad daylight, like a drama on stage, lighted for the very purpose of being seen. But after hours of careful checking it seemed there had been no audience; no one had heard the shots, seen the wounded man fall, observed anyone running away from the wounded detective, or driving off in a car. The nurse, reporting for duty, who had found Kreevich lying in his own blood on the steps, could only have arrived a minute or two after the shooting, but she hadn't seen anything unusual except the wounded man. It had only been nine-thirty at night. There must have been people on the street. She supposed there had been, but her attention had been riveted on Kreevich. No one came forward. The police had broadcast a special number to call, information to be kept secret, identities kept anonymous. No one had called that special number.

It was just after three in the morning when Quist and Strock arrived at St. Margaret's. They were expected, and a uniformed patrolman took them to Dr. Powell's office on the second floor, where Captain Larsen, Sergeant Kaminski, and a plainclothes detective were going through the stack of files that Kreevich had been studying earlier on.

"Thanks for offering to help," Larsen said to Strock.

"I wish I thought I was going to be helpful," the little detective said. "It's like looking at an old memory book. I'm sure I've been through all this stuff before, five–six years ago."

"But not looking for quite the same thing," Larsen said. "Back then you were trying to find out if Maureen Craven had been in the fire. Now we're trying to connect her with Martine, not necessarily with the fire. These are his hospital records for the last twelve years, dozens of disasters, dozens of injuries, dozens of individual cases. We haven't gotten half through them so far."

"Well, I'll give it a whirl," Strock said. He sat down at the desk, almost hidden behind the piles of papers.

Quist and Larsen moved away to a corner of the office.

"They've moved the lieutenant to a private room," Larsen said. "Tubes, machines, God knows what, to try to keep him alive."

"Any sign that he's conscious?"

"If he's aware of anything, he hasn't shown it."

"I'd like to see him," Quist said. "If there's any chance at all that he knows who's there—a friend might be reassuring, might help."

"I know you'd feel better if you tried," Larsen said. He shrugged. "Why not? Room Six C. I'll phone ahead that you're coming. One of my men, Detective Jordan, is stationed there on the chance that he might come to for a moment, say something, speak a single word that might help."

The hospital corridors were empty except for an occasional nurse, or intern, or orderly. Visiting hours were long over. A man on the elevator was disinclined to take Quist up to the sixth floor until he was told it was "police business."

The door to Six C was standing open a couple of inches. Quist hesitated. From down the hall a loud-speaker was asking for a particular doctor to report somewhere. The atmosphere was cold, impersonal, almost painfully disinfected.

Quist pushed open the door of Six C and went in. A nurse was sitting beside a bed which was covered by what Quist supposed was an oxygen tent. He could see only the outlines of a motionless figure under the tent.

Detective Jordan, a young man with a deadpan face, got up from a chair.

"Mr. Quist?"

"Yes."

150

"I'm Jordan. The captain said you were on the way up. Not much use, I'm afraid. He hasn't stirred since they brought him here." He spoke in a stage whisper. "The nurse is Miss Casper."

"There really isn't any point in whispering," she said in a natural voice. "He doesn't hear anything."

Kreevich was lying on his back, his head bandaged, some kind of rack keeping the covers from touching his body. His eyes were closed. There were plastic tubes inserted in his nose.

"What can you tell me?" Quist asked the nurse.

"It would make more sense for you to talk to one of the doctors," she said. "This is a badly hurt man, Mr. Quist. They removed a bullet from his spine, another from a lung, another that severed an artery in his neck. Six in all, I understand. The other three didn't do so much damage."

"He hasn't responded to anyone yet?"

"He'll be a lucky man if he ever does," the nurse said.

It hurt to look at his friend, Quist found, and it also stirred his anger. Somebody was going to pay for this.

"It's probably out of a story book," he said to the nurse, "but isn't it possible he could hear and still not respond?"

"I think it could be," Miss Casper said. "I've known patients to talk, afterward, about things we hadn't thought they were aware of."

"I want to talk to him," Quist said. "If by any chance it gets through to him at all, he'll know that he's not alone."

"I don't see what possible harm it can do," the nurse said. "An exercise in futility, I'm afraid."

She moved a chair close to the bed and lifted the edge of the plastic tent. "Not long," she said.

151

Kreevich's pallor was almost frightening. One hand lay outside the covers and Quist took it, shocked for a moment by its coldness.

"Mark!" he said. "It's Julian."

Not the remotest flicker of an eyelid, nothing. Jordan had moved to stand just behind Quist, in case there was anything.

"You're going to make it, chum," Quist said. "They got all the junk out of you. Mark? Mark, it's Julian. Did you see anything? Can you put a name to the guy?"

Nothing. It was almost impossible to tell whether Kreevich was breathing; the rack holding the bedding away from his body camouflaged any intake or exhaling of air.

Quist glanced up at Miss Casper, still holding Kreevich's icy hand. "Can I move his hand? Can I apply any pressure to it?"

"Squeeze once for yes, twice for no?" the nurse asked. "We've tried. No reason why you shouldn't."

Quist leaned forward, his mouth very close to Kreevich's bandaged head. He tightened his grip on the icy hand. "Mark, it's Julian. I want so very much to get through to you, chum. Can you hear me? If you can, just squeeze my hand."

Nothing.

"The whole force is out looking for the guy who did this to you, Mark. I'm looking, in my way, too. We need help. We need your help, Mark. Please let me know if you can hear me! Move your hand, the one I'm holding."

No movement.

"Did you find something in Dr. Martine's files?" Nothing. "Was there something in those files we should find, that would point us in the right direction?"

152

Nothing. "Mark, for God's sake, help us to help you!"

Quist let go of Kreevich's hand and stood up. "I think he's dead!" he said, his voice unsteady.

Miss Casper took a stethoscope from a medical table, fitted it to her ears, held the monitor to Kreevich's neck.

"Still with us," she said, after a moment or two. "Faint, but surprisingly regular." She put the stethoscope back on the table. Her mouth was set in a firm, straight line. "This man was investigating the murder of Dr. Martine?"

"Why? You knew the doctor?" Quist asked.

"Every girl in this hospital who isn't cross-eyed knew the doctor," Miss Casper said. She looked down at Kreevich. "I knew he was a cop. I didn't know he was trying to catch Claude Martine's killer. If I had, I might have turned off the life supports."

"How do you mean?"

"The person who blasted Claude Martine deserves a medal, not persecution by the police!"

Quist thought he had rarely heard such bitterness. "The good doctor played games with you, Miss Casper?"

"That is none of your effing business, Mr. Quist!"

"Whoever killed the doctor has gone completely off his rocker, Miss Casper; the doctor, Julia Prentiss, the caretaker of the doctor's building, my friend here. There can be more if we don't find him and stop him."

"I'll contribute to his legal fees!" the nurse said. "Women were just objects to be used by your good doctor. So maybe I was one of them! Fortunately for Claude Martine I don't have the stomach for killing, nor do I have a boy friend who might do it for me!" She drew a deep breath. "It was tried before, you know."

"I don't know," Quist said, and as he spoke he

153

remembered Kreevich mentioning someone who had beaten up the doctor here in the hospital, put him out of action for some time.

"Sally Quill was a nice girl, a good nurse," Miss Casper said. "She fell for Claude Martine's line —promises, all kinds of promises."

"A seduction?" Quist asked.

The nurse's face had turned white as paper. "Sex with Claude was the same thing as rape. He liked it with violence, with pain!" A shudder took over the body inside the white uniform. "Sally was hurt, badly hurt. Claude got some butcher friend of his to take care of her. The result was no kids, no marriage, no future."

"And she had a boy friend who did have a stomach for violence?"

The moment of fierce anger left Miss Casper drained. "It's all in the hospital records, Mr. Quist. His name is Bob Boisnay. He came here, looking for Claude, and he found him, in the men's room down on the main floor. It looked like there'd been a pigsticking when three or four orderlies finally put a stop to it."

"Knife?"

Miss Casper shook her head. "He just beat the hell out of Claude. He'd have gone right on beating him till he was dead if he hadn't been stopped. Claude was in the hospital for six weeks—broken jaw, broken nose, broken ribs. Another six weeks recuperating somewhere before he was seen around here again. There's something you won't find in the records, Mr. Quist."

"Oh?"

"Claude Martine never preferred any kind of charges against Sally's guy. The hospital could have had Bob Boisnay for property damage, but I guess Claude talked them out of that; he may have paid for the damages himself."

154

"Why do suppose Martine was willing to let this Boisnay get away with it?"

Miss Casper shrugged. "This was only about a year ago, Mr. Quist. Claude had a big, rich, private practice, ninety percent of his patients women. If Boisnay spoke his piece in court it would have wrecked Claude's practice. You know the first thing I thought when I heard what had happened to Claude and Julia Prentiss on my TV at home? All that stuff about the politician who found them and maybe he was the killer? I didn't buy that. I found myself wondering if Claude had been nosing around Sally Quill again. This time Bob Boisnay wouldn't have let him live!"

"Surely Martine wouldn't have gone back after Sally Quill," Quist said. "He had the field to play."

"So there are probably a dozen other Bob Boisnays around with a gut hatred for Claude," Miss Casper said.

Quist looked down at the motionless body on the bed. Was this a line of inquiry that Kreevich was following in Dr. Powell's office?

"I heard there was a girl who bore Martine a child," Quist said. "I understand he lost a paternity suit and was hooked for child support."

"That's six or seven years ago," Miss Casper said. "Mildred Bellows was a nurse here, too. It was the old story of Claude and his promises. That time he was forced to keep them I guess. But I feel sorry for Mildred. Every time she looks at her six-year-old boy she must wonder if she's brought another monster like Claude Martine into the world."

Quist sat down beside the bed again and covered Kreevich's ice cold hand with his. Could his friend be hearing any of this, unable to let them know?

"One thing puzzles me," he said to Miss Casper. "You've been describing a man who went after any attractive woman who crossed his path. This thing with Sally Quill and Boisnay, you say, was only a year ago. But Julia Prentiss had apparently been living with him for a good deal longer than that. She must have known about Sally Quill, and about others."

Miss Casper's laugh was bitter. "Our little Julia was a business woman. Oh, she went through the usual with Claude, I suppose, but then she became his business partner."

"In his practice?"

"Don't be naive, Mr. Quist. Getting into bed with most women was a way for Claude to get into their bank accounts. So he got a big fee for lifting a face, but that wasn't all he lifted. He collected secrets, and he got paid for keeping his mouth shut about them. Julia kept the records and shared in the profits. Damn it, Mr. Quist, you've made me talk too much!"

"You've helped me lift a few window shades, Miss Casper. I'm grateful." He bent down and spoke, urgently, to the silent figure on the bed. "Stay in there pitching, chum," he said. "I'll be back. I promise."

There was no movement, no response of any sort.

"Blackmail on a big scale," Captain Larsen said when he'd heard Quist's account of Miss Casper's angry remarks.

They were in Dr. Powell's office. George Strock was at the desk, a pile of folders pushed to one side, another in front of him. He had listened to Quist's story, polishing his glasses.

"I've always thought doctors and lawyers would make the world's greatest blackmailers," he said. "Privileged information is the way to the safety deposit boxes."

"Pretty cynical, George," Quist said.

"Maybe," Strock said, fitting his glasses back on his nose. "But since most doctors and lawyers are ethical men, the few bad apples in the barrel must clean up big. Looks like our Dr. Martine was one of them."

"It looked like blackmail or extortion from the start," Captain Larsen said. "Bart Craven, a millionaire, is a prime target; but also a man who has been goaded beyond endurance for seven years. Threatened with some kind of exposure about his late wife, he just couldn't take it anymore."

"Or he's telling the truth and he didn't get to Martine's house in time to hear whatever it was Martine planned to tell him. Someone with a killing grudge got to the doctor first."

George Strock reached for the file folder on the top of the pile he hadn't yet attacked. "We all go to our own different churches. You're after a killer, Captain. Mr. Quist is trying to defend a client. Me? The only thing that really fascinates me is what Dr. Martine had to tell Craven about his wife. I've spent six years and found nothing. What did I miss?" He opened the folder in front of him. "Going different ways, we all may meet at the same barbecue."

The nurse in Six C had started Quist down a new path, looking for a new light at the end. For two days now they had been backtracking on Maureen Craven, hoping to find an answer to a seven-year-old tragedy. Miss Casper's dirt on Dr. Martine suggested another approach, another angle. A very early theory had been that the killer, not connected with either Bart or Maureen Craven, had got to the doctor and his partner in crime in the forty minutes between the phone call to Bart and Bart's arrival at the office. If Miss Casper was right about Dr. Martine's nonprofessional approach to big money, there could be a whole army of people who had lived in fear of him, and hated him enough to wipe him out.

"And they won't be eager to talk to the police while the murders are unsolved, because they all could be suspects," Quist said to Captain Larsen. They had left Strock in Dr. Powell's office and gone down the hall to the coffee machine in the staff room.

"And not too willing to help in any case," Larsen said.

"Miss Casper talked about contributing to legal fees of anyone who was charged with murder," Quist said. "She hated Martine that much. There are others who join her in that feeling, I imagine."

"What's on your mind?"

"To talk to Bob Boisnay and his girl friend, and to Mildred Bellows, who mothered Martine's son. I'm trying to protect a friend of mine from being charged with Martine's murder. They might be willing to talk, tell me something that could be useful."

"And clam up to a policeman?"

"Right. I don't want to get in your way, so I need your okay," Quist said.

"I guess we can dig up addresses for you," Larsen said.

Six o'clock on a winter morning, still dark, is not a normal time to go calling on a stranger. Robert Boisnay lived in an apartment in an old brownstone on Jane Street in Greenwich Village. Quist stood in the vestibule with his finger on the button marked Boisnay. After what seemed an interminable time, a man's angry voice came through the intercom speaker.

"Stop ringing the bell, goddamn it! Who are you? What do you want?"

"Mr. Boisnay?"

"You're expecting maybe Jimmy Carter?"

"My name is Quist. It may not mean anything to you, but I need to talk to you about Dr. Martine."

There was a silence. The voice from upstairs turned cold. "You police?"

"No. If you've followed the case—and I'm sure you have—you've probably heard me mentioned as a friend of Bart Craven's."

"Public relations man!"

"Right."

"What do you want from me?"

"Talk. My friend needs help, Boisnay. I wouldn't be here at this time of day if it wasn't urgent."

"Ring the bell again in five minutes," Boisnay said.

Quist waited, stamping his feet to keep them warm against the freezing cold. He rang the bell again and the clicking sound came, releasing the front door lock. Quist stepped into the dimly lighted hallway.

"Second floor," a voice called down the stairwell to him.

On the landing above the two men faced each other, the tall, blond, elegant Quist, and Boisnay, dark, intense, almost boyish.

"This had better make sense, Mr. Quist," Boisnay said.

"I hope it will."

"Come in." Boisnay opened the nearest door and stood aside.

Quist walked into a small, almost cramped-looking living room. A table lamp provided the only light. Shades were drawn down over the two windows. It was hard to tell, from a quick look around, what kind of person or people lived here.

"I ought to have my head examined for letting you

up," Boisnay said. "A stranger—in the middle of the night!"

"Can I take off my coat and sit for a minute?" Quist asked.

"You've come this far. Since you must know about me to have come here, Quist, I don't know what else there is I can tell you. That chair is not apt to collapse under you."

Quist put his topcoat on a bench by the front door and sat down in the chair Boisnay indicated. Bright black eyes watched every move he made.

"I've been waiting for the cops to come," Boisnay said. "When I heard that sonofabitch was dead and that maybe your boy, Craven, didn't kill him, I figured the Homicide boys would get around to everybody who ever had trouble with him. I'd be at the top of their list." He turned his head and Quist saw a slender, blond girl, wearing a maroon-colored flannel bathrobe, standing in what he guessed was the doorway to a small kitchen.

"I've put on coffee, Bob," she said.

"This is my lady, Sally Quill," Boisnay said.

Quist stood up to acknowledge the introduction. This pale girl had been one of Martine's victims.

"I don't have to stay, Bob," the girl said. "I'll just bring the coffee when it's ready."

"Stay!" Boisnay said. He sounded harsh, but he reached out a hand to the girl and she came quickly to him, knelt on the floor beside his chair, her head against his knee. He stroked her hair. It was a gesture of tenderness. "'Curiosity killed the cat,' my old lady used to say," he said. "So I let you come up here, Quist."

It required going back over old territory, the last two days, the last seven years.

"So I have a double interest in the case," Quist said

finally. "I want to find Bart Craven and clear him, and I want to find the man who shot my friend Mark Kreevich and make certain he gets nailed to the nearest barn door."

"And how do you think I could help—if I would?" Boisnay asked. "You're thinking kind of funny, aren't you? What makes you think Sally and I didn't have a celebration when we heard that bastard was dead? Why do you think we'd help you to trip up the guy who succeeded where I failed about fourteen months ago?"

"You meant to kill Martine?"

"You're damn right. Only I didn't have a plan. I was just going to beat his brains out."

"Because of what he did to Miss Quill?"

"See about the coffee, babe," Boisnay said to the girl. She jumped up and hurried into the kitchen. "I had her just about forgetting it till all this murder stuff started coming over the tube. I don't want you asking her questions, stirring it all up again."

"Almost the last thing Martine did before he was shot," Quist said, "was to call Bart Craven and tell him he knew what had happened to his wife seven years ago. It seems obvious to me that that was a preliminary to blackmail. It has thrown a good man into shock, wrecked his future, his career. If blackmail was a sideline with Martine, and I believe it was, then right at this moment there are undoubtedly other people on the ropes, frightened, waiting for the police to dig up some secret they've paid to keep hidden. One of those people may be the killer, but he's gone beyond anything for which we can, remotely, feel any sympathy. I can understand why you might not want to help me trip up whoever killed Martine and his girl. But what about the caretaker who just went to see why a light was burning in

161

the middle of the night? What about my friend Lieutenant Kreevich, who was gunned down because he might be on the trail of something?"

"Was he?"

"I don't know. He hasn't talked, can't talk, may never talk."

"According to the tube the person who shot the caretaker was searching the house. Looking for *his* secret? Whatever it was Martine had on him?"

"A good guess, I think."

"But didn't find it?"

"Why go after Kreevich if he had?"

Boisnay sat scowling down at the toes of his shoes. Sally Quill appeared from the kitchen, carrying three mugs of coffee on a small tray.

"Sugar? Cream?" she asked Quist.

"Fine the way it is," he said.

She stood silent for a moment, looking at the two men.

"I think I should tell Mr. Quist something, Bob," she said.

"You don't have to get involved. Just stay out of it, babe," Boisnay said.

She put her hand on Boisnay's shoulder. "I think he should know," she said. "I was a nurse at St. Margaret's, Mr. Quist. A probationer, just starting. There'd been an explosion at an oil refinery, somewhere in Jersey, and six or seven badly burned people were brought in. That was the first time Dr. Martine came into my picture. I heard all the gossip about him from the other nurses. He was a woman-chaser, a bad boy. Then I was put on night duty caring for one of the burn patients. The girls warned me to look out for Martine. He was flirtatious for a couple of nights, actually made some outright

162

suggestions. It didn't bother me. I wasn't interested. I had Bob."

"You don't have to talk!" Boisnay almost shouted.

"I used to hear, when I was a kid, that there was no way a man could rape a woman unless she was halfway willing. She had ways to protect herself."

"Sally!" Boisnay protested.

"Well, it's not true, Mr. Quist. Not if the man is a rape-queer. Not if he doesn't need a response from the woman to make it. I was handled like a rag doll, beaten, violated, hurt!" Her voice trembled. "You don't want to tell when something like that happens to you, not anyone. I couldn't tell Bob. I knew what he'd do. But I was in trouble, internal injuries. I was hemorrhaging. I didn't know who to go to without telling the whole thing. Believe it or not I—I went to him, to Dr. Martine. He acted as if he were really distressed. I guess he didn't want me to talk any more than I wanted to. He sent me to a doctor friend of his and I think that doctor did everything he could for me. But the result was—was the end for me. I'd never be a whole woman again. I . . . I . . ."

"She tried to break off with me," Boisnay said.

"The reason I'm telling you all this, Mr. Quist," Sally Quill said, "is that we never knew anything about any blackmail. The night I told Bob he took off for the hospital, and . . ."

"I was going to kill him!" Boisnay said. "Then, after I was arrested, it turned out he wouldn't bring charges against me. Everybody knew why I did what I did, but the law never came into it. I guess Dr. Powell was kind of in on it with Martine. I did a couple of hundred bucks worth of damage in that men's room, but I wasn't asked to make good. Martine, through his lawyer, a man

163

named Wilshire, offered me money to keep my mouth shut. I told him to shove it! But, when I cooled down, I knew I wasn't going to talk on account of Sally."

"And that was that?"

"Not exactly," Boisnay said. "I was never going to let up on the creep. I was going to catch him in some way that didn't involve Sally and let him have it—let the whole damn world know what kind of guy he was. So—so I've made a kind of study of him. Only somebody got him before I could."

"There was a girl who bore him a son," Quist said.

"Oh, that was public knowledge, a court case. Girl's name was Mildred Bellows."

"Another nurse at the hospital?"

"No. A patient, I think. She'd been willing enough to have a thing with Martine, I guess. But when she got pregnant she made him pay. He moved them out to the Southwest somewhere—Tucson, Phoenix, some place like that. Out of his local bailiwick."

"The paternity suit didn't damage him? Professionally, I mean?"

"In this day and age, Mr. Quist? Probably made him more interesting to the gals who are in and out of his office, getting their faces fixed and their appetite for sex satisfied."

"So what did your study of Dr. Martine tell you?"

"That he was a hell of a lot richer than even his extravagant fees could make him," Boisnay said. "It had to come from all the rich ladies he serviced—medically I mean. He couldn't play stud to all of them and keep them happy, so it had to be something else. Secrets, I told myself. He was making a business of secrets. Julia Prentiss was in on it with him, for sure. But there was someone else, a man who drives a Mercedes, has a country house and a city house, and made quiet deals

164

for the doctor. Wilshire, the lawyer. I spent quite a little time on Stuart Wilshire. Would you believe, for all the dough he obviously has, he handles almost no court cases, and the customers aren't lined up outside his office? I'll tell you something he did do. Three, four nights a week, after office hours, he visited that house of Martine's on Thirty-eighth Street. I don't think he went there to play backgammon. Maybe he drew up wills for rich women. Maybe he kept Martine informed on how deeply he could put the hook into some poor lame-brained female."

"Three people on a blackmailing team, you're saying?"

"Big business," Boisnay said. "I've got to say one good thing about Martine, Mr. Quist. He was one hell of a doctor, and I don't think he ever gave a hospital patient, or a private patient, for that matter, less than the best of his skill, his care, his medical attention. What he did with the rest of their lives is another story. The point I'm making is that his work as a doctor was time consuming. When there was one of those emergencies at St. Margaret's, it was round the clock, sometimes for days. So to handle another big business he required help."

"He had Julia Prentiss."

"Yeah, and he also had a lawyer who visited him during the week, after hours. How much pressure can you put on a certain victim without getting into legal trouble? A lawyer could tell you. But take another look at it, Mr. Quist. Someone searched that house, upstairs and down according to the papers, after Martine was killed."

"And shot the caretaker when he found him there."

"And later your cop friend. It seems like that guy didn't find what he was looking for in that house. And come to think of it, why should he?" Boisnay asked.

"What would a blackmailer have? Letters? Pictures? Or maybe tapes of conversations on a bugged telephone, or from a microphone hidden under a bed? A physical thing, I mean, small, not a trunk. According to the tube, the killer was looking in bureau drawers, desk drawers, the pockets of suits, file cabinets. Places to hide a small object."

"So?"

"He didn't find it because it wasn't there. Come to think of it, why should it be? Why would Martine keep incriminating stuff in a place where people are in and out all day, 'WALK-IN' painted on the door? He had this lawyer with a fancy office, probably a safe there. I'll make you a small bet, Mr. Quist, that Stuart Wilshire, attorney-at-law, has all the material for carrying on a one-man business now. He won't have to split with anyone!"

Quist looked thoughtfully at Boisnay. "Could Wilshire have killed his partners, seeing where the profit lay?"

"Why not?" Boisnay said. "There's one thing he wouldn't have, you know, which might explain why he searched the house. What did Martine have on him? You can be sure Martine wouldn't have a partner, who knew all about his criminal activities, without having something to keep him in line! Martine would keep that hidden somewhere in his own house."

"You're an interesting man, Boisnay," Quist said. "I think I'd like to catch up with Stuart Wilshire and see what he's like."

"He was a friend of Martine's," Boisnay said. "You can count on it he'll smell bad."

Stuart Wilshire, attorney-at-law, wasn't easy to reach at seven o'clock in the morning. He had an unlisted number at his home, wherever that might be, and the phone at his Park Avenue office went unanswered. The police had no home address for him, nor did Miss Taylor, Martine's receptionist, who was awakened out of her beauty sleep by Quist's telephone call.

"If Dr. Martine had a private number he kept it to himself," she told Quist. "I have a book of unlisted numbers at the office—patients, doctor friends—Mr. Wilshire isn't among them. A couple of times, I remember, he asked me to call Mr. Wilshire's office and ask him to get in touch. He laughed and said, 'Stuart is a night person. Even his secretary doesn't get in till ten o'clock. Don't bother to call before then.' "

Quist went home to his own apartment and covered his other bases while Lydia made him some breakfast. He'd almost lost track of the order of things, whether it was breakfast or dinner time. At the hospital the report on Kreevich was static. No significant change, one way or the other. An anxious Rachel Hoyt had no news of Bart.

"This is longer than it's ever been, Mr. Quist. Do you think . . ."

"I think Bart's working out his own problem, Rachel. If anything had happened to him we'd know."

"That's what he always said about Maureen—he'd know if she wasn't alive somewhere."

And the poor guy was still believing that, Quist thought. If Rachel hadn't heard, there was little chance that Dilys Johns or Jack Milburn had. They asked, politely, about Kreevich. There was nothing on Bart.

"Back in those days when Bart was abroad, that last month when you were keeping an eye on Maureen, did you ever drop in at a place called the Fairmount for a drink?" Quist asked Jack Milburn.

"Where?"

"The Fairmount, the hotel that burned down the night Maureen disappeared. I wondered if it was a place she might have gone on her own? It was just about three blocks from her apartment."

"Oh, sure, I remember," Milburn said. "Missing Persons made a thing of it at the time. I was never in the place in my life. It was kind of a dump, as I recall. I certainly never heard Maureen mention it. She didn't go to places alone to drink. Drinking was purely social with her, not a necessity. She wouldn't go to a place like the Fairmount to drink when she was only three blocks from her own home. Why do you ask?"

"It came up again, checking over the old Missing Persons records."

"They were just reaching for anything back then," Milburn said.

"You ever hear of a man named Stuart Wilshire?"

"No. Who's he?"

"Dr. Martine's lawyer."

"For God's sake, Julian, I never heard of Dr. Martine until two nights ago, when Bart got involved."

"He told Bart he knew something about Maureen. It just happens he took care of the burn victims from that Fairmount fire."

"Missing Persons told Bart, at the time, that everyone in that fire was accounted for except one woman. Bart gave them Maureen's dental chart, medical history. The dead woman wasn't Maureen. I haven't thought about it from that day till now. Is there still some question, Julian?"

Quist felt very tired. "The woods are full of questions," he said, "but damn few answers. The police think if Martine really did know something about Maureen it must go back to the time when she was still alive, still around. You can't blackmail a dead person. Martine goes back seven years with her, or he has a patient who goes back seven years with her."

"I wish I knew how to help," Milburn said.

"I wish you did, friend," Quist said. "I sure as hell wish you did." He was thinking of Kreevich's dead white face, and that cold hand resting on the bed covers.

Lydia had coffee, bacon and eggs, and a toasted English muffin for him. She waited till he had finished eating and reached for a pipe and a roll-up pouch on the bookcase next to the table to give him news she was sure he expected.

"Senator Metzger called once more, Julian. He has been persuaded to run again. Would you convey his regrets to Bart—and know how sorry he is that the campaign that Julian Quist Associates were engaged to promote is off. He wishes that he might have you working on his team, but under the circumstances . . ."

"Bart's friends are now beyond the pale," Quist said without anger.

She passed him a table lighter for his pipe. "I wish you'd back off, Julian, and leave this whole mess to the police. You had an obligation to Bart's campaign, but he's not your close friend."

"Mark is," Quist said, holding the lighter to his pipe. He took a couple of drags on it and put it down on the table beside his not quite finished breakfast. This morning nothing gave him the pleasure it was meant to give him.

"You'll just be making yourself a target for a psychopath," Lydia said. "It won't help Mark for you to become a victim too."

"You been talking to Jack Milburn?" he asked.

"No."

"Because that's his theory." He got up and walked over to the windows that looked down at the ice-clogged

169

waters of the East River. "If I was in Mark's place, lying there in the hospital, would you back off?"

"You know I wouldn't, love. But there are people trained to do certain things." She came to stand by him, her arm slipped through his. "While Bart's future was still at stake, finding him, talking some sense to him, was something you could possibly do. Now it doesn't matter when he turns up. Let Rachel, or Dilys, or Jack Milburn handle that part of it. Let the police, who are trained to handle violence, deal with that part of it. You know how total their commitment will be to finding the man who's hurt one of their own."

He turned, bent down, and kissed her on one cheek and then the other. "People are my business, Lydia, judging them, assessing them, maneuvering them. This kid Boisnay had some pretty shrewd notions about Martine's lawyer."

"Wilshire?"

"Yes. I'm going to go talk to him when he gets to his office. I may come up empty, I may come up with something. I know damn well Mark was on the trail of something. Maybe George Strock and Larsen will find it in those files at the hospital, but it can take hours and hours for them to get through all that stuff."

"Mark found it in two hours if he found anything," Lydia said.

"But he knew what he was looking for. Stuart Wilshire was close to Martine. He probably knows more about him than anyone we know of who's left alive. Except Mark, who may never tell us!"

"If he's a villain, he isn't going to tell you anything."

"It depends on what's to his advantage," Quist said. "I'm going that far, Lydia. After that—well, we can talk again."

"I'm so damned frightened for you, Julian!"

170

"I'm a little scared myself," he said. "But Mark's got to have somebody fighting for him."

"He's got the whole police force!"

He smiled at her. "Maybe they're not as smart as I am," he said.

3

The Park Avenue building where Stuart Wilshire had his office was new, modern, smelled of rich tenants. Wilshire's name was on the board in the lobby, twenty-fourth floor. Lobby attendants were smartly uniformed.

His name was on the door of the office—STUART WILSHIRE, COUNSELOR-AT-LAW. Quist walked in. Thick rugs, expensive paintings, windows looking out over the towers on the city. A dark-haired girl sat at a flat-topped desk.

"May I help you?" she asked.

"I want to see Mr. Wilshire," Quist said.

"I know you don't have an appointment with him," the girl said. "If you'll give me your name perhaps I can arrange one for you."

"I want to see him now. You can tell him my name is Julian Quist and I want to talk to him about Dr. Martine."

That hit her where she lived, he thought. She hesitated a moment, and before she could decide what to do a door at the far end of the room opened and a well-dressed, grey-haired man stood there.

"The miracle of modern electronics, Mr. Quist," he said. "An intercom system which Miss Lacey keeps open

171

when strangers appear. Come in, won't you? I'm Stuart Wilshire."

The inner office was what Quist expected: a calf-bound law library, a carved antique desk, comfortable leather armchairs. The bright winter sky was visible through a big window at the far end of the room. Wilshire gestured to a chair and sat down behind his desk.

"I've been wondering why nobody's come to see me, Mr. Quist," Wilshire said. "I hadn't expected it to be you, but here you are."

"You know who I am?"

"Of course. If you look out the window there, you'll see the building that houses the offices of Julian Quist Associates, public relations. You were planning to run a political campaign for Bart Craven. I've just heard on the news that Senator Metzger is going to run again. That means your horse is scratched, doesn't it?"

"Yes."

"I don't know what it is you think I can do for you, Mr. Quist, but I couldn't resist satisfying my curiosity."

This was not a man, Quist thought, who was likely to fall for a sucker punch. The faint smile, the hint of humor in the grey eyes, suggested someone who enjoyed playing whatever game he was involved in. He radiated self-assurance.

"I don't imagine I have to bring you up to date on anything that has to do with the murder of your client, Dr. Martine," Quist said.

"I don't imagine you do, Mr. Quist."

"Except, perhaps, that the Homicide detective who was shot outside St. Margaret's last night is a close, personal friend."

"Lieutenant Kreevich? Is there news of his condition?"

"Critical."

"The last I heard he had not named anyone."

"He hasn't. He may not."

"That bad?"

"Yes."

The two men sat studying each other.

"Well, Mr. Quist?" Wilshire said.

"I know the obstacle to your telling me anything I might want to know," Quist said. "Client-lawyer relationship."

The little smile widened slightly. "That rule sometimes bends a little when the client is dead," Wilshire said. "As a lawyer I am also an officer of the court. I'm also interested in seeing my late client's murderer brought to justice."

"I'm glad to hear that, because he has murdered three people, and maybe four. He could go on and on."

"The police think they're dealing with a psycho?"

"Don't you?"

"It has the earmarks." Again the smile. "Are you here to ask me if I list any psychos among my clients or friends?"

Quist leaned forward. "Mr. Wilshire, I know what a fine doctor and expert surgeon your client was. I've also come to believe that he was a high-powered blackmailer."

"Oh, come now, Mr. Quist. Based on what evidence?" The smiling face revealed nothing.

"It is going to be possible, Mr. Wilshire, to go down the list of Dr. Martine's patients—we have files and files of them—and talk to them. Sooner or later, somewhere, the dam will break and the truth will come out. Women who have been paying and paying will realize that they're safe now. Both the doctor and his nurse, who knew all his secrets, are dead. When one talks, others

173

will talk. But it can take a lot of time to reach that breakdown point, and meanwhile a crazy killer can keep killing."

"And if I were to tell you, 'Yes, Claude was a blackmailer,' how would that get you to the killer?"

"That isn't what I was going to ask you to tell me," Quist said. "Because whether you say yes or no I'm already convinced."

"Just out of thin air?"

"Perhaps, although I'm certain we'll prove it in the long run. My 'thin air' has some substance to it. You know that, forty minutes before he was found dead, Martine called Bart Craven to tell him he had information about his wife's disappearance seven years ago. Doesn't that smell like blackmail to you, Mr. Wilshire?"

"Or compassion," Wilshire said. "He'd stumbled across some information that would relieve a man who'd lived in torture for seven years."

"I've come across nothing that suggests he was a compassionate man. There is Sally Quill, and Mildred Bellows, and nurses at the hospital who shudder when his name is mentioned."

The smile turned rueful. "He could be a bad boy with women."

"And women were his life, professionally and in private. He doctored them, he forced himself on them, and I think he bled the rich ones."

"You expect me to have records of those bleedings here in my office?"

"What did he know about Maureen Craven?"

Wilshire actually laughed. "Are you suggesting that Claude shared his blackmail materials with me, Mr. Quist?"

"The thought had occurred to me."

"Well, now, perhaps I shouldn't find myself so

amused. Make that suggestion publicly, Mr. Quist, and you could find yourself in rather serious legal difficulties."

"I know, for example, that it was a routine of yours, Mr. Wilshire, to visit Dr. Martine at his home three or four nights a week. Was it as a patient? Just socially, as a friend? Or did it have to do with Dr. Martine's other business, blackmail?"

"You're walking along the edge of a cliff, Mr. Quist."

"You care to explain?"

The smile remained fixed on the lawyer's face but he was no longer amused. "Yes, I'll explain," he said. "Claude Martine's practice was very special, most unusual. Much of it was what you might call a luxury business, rich women who couldn't bear to grow old. Cosmetic surgery is the technical name for it. There are no standard fees. It isn't covered by medical insurance, or Medicare, or Medicaid. The doctor charges what the freight will stand. My connection with that was to go into the financial background of prospective patients and arrive at a figure that I thought Claude could charge. This sometimes led to my making a deal with the patient herself, an arrangement for paying over a period of time, so much a month over so many months. Yes, I went to Claude's house in the evening—perhaps not as often as you suggest, but a couple of times a week. He would have for me the names and significant data on new patients. I would have suggestions for him on what to charge patients we'd talked about the last time."

"You're talking about a lot of money."

"Of course. That's no secret. Several hundred thousand dollars a year. There was nothing criminal about it, Mr. Quist. He paid his debts, he paid his taxes."

"And for the support of an illegitimate child?"

"That, I guess, you would have to call a personal and

private mistake which became public knowledge and for which he paid the penalty the court required. That you might call blackmail, but Claude was the victim, not the blackmailer."

"And so you have financial records on hundreds of women patients?"

"Yes. I do. Ten years of private practice, with many of these highly specialized operations a year. But let me tell you something, Mr. Quist. If the police asked to see those records I'd tell them to drop dead. I'd tell Internal Revenue Service the same thing. They can find the list of Claude's patients in his files. They can dig out information on their finances just the way I did. Hard work. And, incidentally, if you ask me to see those records I will tell you just where to put that request."

Quist glanced around the office. "You must have done pretty well, representing Dr. Martine."

"And others, Mr. Quist, quite a few others. I collected a percentage from Claude on each one of his surgical fees that I helped to set up, to arrange. I did very nicely, thank you, and I may tell you that information is in the hands of the IRS. I pay my taxes, too."

"We've wandered away from the question, Mr. Wilshire. What did Dr. Martine know about Maureen Craven?"

Wilshire leaned back in his chair, tips of his fingers pressed together. "The only questions I could answer, if I chose to, would relate to patients whose fees I helped to set. Maureen Craven was not one of them."

"You can be that sure without checking back on your records, checking back seven years?"

The smile returned. "Of course not, Mr. Quist, but I've had two days to check back. Nowhere, in the ten years that I've represented Claude Martine, do I find the name Craven. I heard and read accounts of the murders night before last, and of Craven's explanation of why he was there. It was automatic for me to check back, although it didn't ring any bells."

"You'd never heard of Maureen?"

"I didn't say that. Anybody who was living in New York seven years ago has heard about her. I even remember talking to Claude about her at the time." Wilshire held up his hand. "Don't get hopeful, Mr. Quist. There was a fire at a cheap little fleabag hotel somewhere downtown on the same day Maureen Craven disappeared. Burn victims were brought to St. Margaret's where Claude headed up the burn unit emergency service. A week or so later Missing Persons tried to make certain that Maureen Craven wasn't among the victims. They talked to Claude, who'd examined both the living and the dead. It was all in the papers and on TV. Naturally, Claude and I mentioned it casually. He was quite certain Mrs. Craven wasn't one of the victims. That was all. And she certainly wasn't a patient I was asked to check on later."

"She may have had quite a bit of money," Quist said. "Dr. Martine seems to have had an appetite for money."

"Let me tell you something about Claude Martine," Wilshire said. "You're right, he was a greedy man. Money represented power, and luxury, and security to him. He wanted them all. But he was first and foremost a doctor—a doctor with a sideline that made him rich. I have watched him work through one of these disaster situations where people were terribly burned. That became a medical challenge for him, not a way to inflate his bank account. His pride, his skills were involved. I have known him to work for weeks and months on some of those victims, trying to repair them to the point where they looked like human beings again, trying to get them to a point where they could function with something approaching normalcy. *And not take one red cent for his services!"*

"There was the Texas millionaire."

"One out of hundreds. I suggested earlier he may have called Craven out of compassion. You thought I was making a joke. Claude was really two people. One side of the coin was a man with enormous compassion and sympathy for the sick, the injured, the desperate whom he could help with his medical skills. On the other side was a cynic with a contempt for the vain old women who paid him well for removing their wrinkles and their double chins. He would go way out on a limb for someone in trouble, but he had no use for vanity even though it helped to make him rich."

"How does any of that relate to Maureen Craven?"

"No idea," Wilshire said. A little light blinked on the phone on his desk. He made a polite apology, picked up the phone and said, "Yes?" He listened for a moment and then turned to Quist, his eyebrows raised. "It seems to be for you, Mr. Quist. You make an answering service out of my telephone?"

It had to be Lydia. She was the only person who knew where Quist was.

"What is it, love?" he asked.

She sounded tense. "There's just been a call from Nadine Connors," Lydia said. "She says she may have heard from Maureen Craven."

"She *what?*"

"I'm quoting her exactly, Julian. She said, 'I may have heard from Maureen. I'm badly frightened, Miss Morton, and the only people I know to turn to are you and Mr. Quist.' She's on her way here now, Julian."

"I'm on my horse," he said.

The only time Quist had seen Nadine Connors was in her role in the comedy at the Stetson Theater, and later in her dressing room, her face smeared with cold cream. On stage she had been handsome, but lights and makeup could have accounted for that. Now, in his apartment, Quist saw a smartly dressed, really beautiful woman in her mid-seventies, the lines at the corners of her eyes and mouth somehow adding to her dignity and her charm. Quist was reminded of the late Gladys Cooper, another English actress, who had grown lovelier as she aged.

Miss Connors was badly shaken. Poise and control, a part of her professional technique, her posture for the world which was always her audience, on or offstage, had slipped. She was sitting in a chair in his living room gripping the chair arms as though she thought she or it might take off. Lydia was standing by her. She'd offered a brandy which the lady hadn't touched.

"It's not to be believed, Mr. Quist!" she said.

"Take it easy, Miss Connors."

"Dear God, how do you take it easy when you may have heard from the dead?" She struggled for control. "I was in my room, in my bed, in the hotel when my phone rang. I lie in bed rather late when it isn't a matinee day. Eight shows a week—but why am I wasting time with that? I answered the phone, a little annoyed that the switchboard had put the call through. They told me later that 'the gentleman had said it was an emergency.' That's how it sounded, like a man with some kind of throat trouble, like a prize fighter who's been hit too often on the Adam's apple. 'Nadine?' this hoarse voice asked. 'Who is this?' I asked back. And then the voice said, 'It's Maureen.' I was shocked, of course, but I didn't believe it. I said something like, 'I am not fond of practical jokes!'" Miss Connors drew a deep

179

breath. "Then she said, 'Patricia Blank in the convent pageant.' That was her name before I got her into films, you know."

"That's not a secret from anyone who wanted to play a cruel joke on you," Quist said. "The story of her original name, given to her by the nuns, was in hundreds of press releases when she was at the top."

"Then she said, 'The pink dress you bought me when you took me from the convent to the film studio.' Well, I had bought her a pink dress. I remember it very well. She looked stunning in it. 'Your dog's name was Petrucio,' she said. Oh God, Mr. Quist, I had a little Welch corgi in those days who went everywhere with me, and his name was Petrucio. 'You're not Maureen,' I said. 'I would know Maureen's voice anywhere.' And she said, in that awful croaking sound, 'I don't have a voice any more, Nadine. Please listen to me! Please!' I don't mean to sound melodramatic, Mr. Quist, but it was a cry for help out of hell somewhere."

"Just take it slowly, Miss Connors."

"Then she told me she was in some kind of terrible trouble, that she hadn't known anybody to turn to but me. I suggested that if she were really Maureen, she had a husband, close friends, the police. 'I need help, advice, before I go to any of them. Please come to me, Nadine! Please!' It didn't make any sense, Mr. Quist. If this voice belonged to Maureen, if it was real, why me? 'If you bring the police with you that will be the end,' she said. 'One policeman is already dying. I need help to save lives, Nadine. Will you come?' I said it would take me some time, but I would. I was already thinking of you and Miss Morton. She gave me an address. It's on the Lower East Side, somewhere." Miss Connors fumbled in her handbag and handed a slip of paper to Quist. A

180

number on Second Avenue was written on it. "Then she said, 'When you get here, Nadine, be prepared for a pretty stiff jolt. I'm not as you remember me.' So I called you, Mr. Quist, because I don't know what to do."

Lydia looked at her man. "Call Captain Larsen," she said.

He sat staring at the old actress, as if he hoped to read something there that hadn't come out in her conversation.

"That doctor who was killed must really have known something," Miss Connors said. "Will you go with me, Mr. Quist? I just don't have the courage to try it alone. Yet, somehow, I believe it was for real, not some kind of wicked game."

"You think it was Maureen?" Quist asked.

"It's not possible, is it? But . . . yes!"

"Then I'll go with you," Quist said.

"And *I'll* call Captain Larsen," Lydia said.

"You'll just sit tight and do nothing for a spell," Quist said. He slipped an arm around her shoulders. She was trembling.

"Bart Craven answered a phone call," she said.

"I know. The chances are that if this is Maureen—or even if it's someone playing games—when Miss Connors arrives with someone from the police, we won't get any further than that. But if there's a chance of learning something—well, this person knows about Kreevich being shot. If we can be told who . . ."

Lydia turned away. When Quist had made up his mind she knew there was no diverting him. It was insanity for him to go off with this old lady into what had to be a trap. But he would go.

The day itself was reassuring, the sun bright and warm for January, last night's snow shower forgotten, melted away. It was hard to believe that they were heading through this sunlit healthiness toward something that might be dark and evil.

It was going on noon when Quist and Nadine Connors started downtown in a taxi toward the Second Avenue address. The actress sat, rigid, in her corner of the seat.

"I'm a bloody coward," she said. "If I was prepared to help Maureen, why couldn't I do it her way, go alone, not involve anyone else?"

"She said police. I'm not police. I'm her husband's friend."

"I wonder if that's a recommendation, Mr. Quist? If we're headed for Maureen, if she's really alive, she's spent seven years *not* contacting her husband, their friends, people she surely could trust."

"Trust with what?" Quist asked, sounding far away. Whoever the caller was, she had known about Kreevich, suggested there might be still more. Anyone watching television or listening to the radio would know all that, but not anyone who watched or listened would have known of the connection between Maureen and Nadine Connors unless they had studied the old case of seven years ago, the disappearance of Bart Craven's young wife. Two days ago Dr. Martine had revived that old story with his call to Bart; now this, today, another revival.

"Do you realize, Mr. Quist, that I haven't been in New York for seven years?" Miss Connors said. "Not since that month when Mr. Craven was in the Middle East. I saw Maureen quite often for a week. I went on to the Coast then for my film and never heard from her again. If she was alive and in trouble, and if I was someone she thought could help her, why wait all this time, seven long years?"

"Maybe we'll find all the answers where we're going," Quist said. "Maybe someone is already laughing at us for being a couple of gullible dummies." He leaned forward and tapped on the glass behind the driver. The man turned and slid the partition open.

"Drop us about a block from the address I gave you," Quist said.

"You got it," the driver said, and closed the partition again.

"I've been careless," Quist said to Miss Connors. "Someone can have been following you, following us from my place. I just didn't check, and there's no way of picking out someone in this traffic now. The address we're headed for may be watched."

"Why?"

"I'm damned if I know, Miss Connors. Why any of this?"

The cab pulled up at a corner curb. "Just about a block south on the west side of the street," the driver told Quist as he was paid off.

Quist glanced at the slip of paper Nadine Connors had given him. "Smith—81½ Second Avenue." He looked up and down the street. No other cab seemed to have stopped close by.

"You stay here, Miss Connors. I'll walk down to the address and check the name plate inside the door. If it's the right place I'll signal you."

"Whatever you say."

"And *watch*, Miss Connors. If anyone seems to be following me . . ."

"I'll dance a hornpipe," the actress said.

It was a block of small residence buildings, small markets, the usual newspaper-stationery-tobacco store, a small movie house with a marquee out over the pavement. KRAMER VS. KRAMER. DUSTIN HOFFMAN.

183

Number 81½ was a narrow, yellow brick building, not old but shabby looking. Two apartments to a floor, front and back, Quist guessed. Four floors. He walked straight past the door. He'd noticed a man on the opposite side of the avenue walking down the sidewalk there, apparently keeping pace with him. When he reached the corner, Quist stopped. The man he'd wondered about kept on going, crossed the intersection, and went on down the avenue without looking back. False alarm.

Quist turned back. He saw Nadine Connors at the far end of the block. She passed her hand across her face in a gesture that suggested "nothing." He walked up the three brick steps and into the narrow vestibule of 81½. There were mailboxes and names—Smith, 3R. All of the apartments were R or F, Rear or Front. No one in 3R could be watching the street from windows.

He went back out onto the street and signaled to Miss Connors. She came toward him, walking briskly. There was nothing that suggested age about this elegant old woman.

"No one seemed interested in you," she said when she reached him.

They went into the vestibule together. They stood looking at Smith, 3R.

"Ready?" Quist asked.

She nodded and he pressed the button. Almost instantly there was the clicking sound of the lock being released. They went into the dark inner hall. From above came a voice, a harsh, croaking voice.

"Nadine?"

"Yes," Miss Connors said, loud and clear. She whispered to Quist. *"It can't be! It just can't be!"*

"Please come up—two flights," the croaking voice called out.

184

Quist and Miss Connors started up, he going first, she following. The stairway and the halls weren't kept clean. There was gum wrappers, a crumpled pack of cigarettes, an accumulation of dust and dirt.

The door to 3R was open an inch or two. Quist guessed there was a chain lock on the inside.

The indescribable voice spoke angrily from behind the opening. "I told you to come alone, Nadine!"

"You told me not to bring the police," Miss Connors said. Whatever she was feeling she sounded cool and quite collected. "This is not a policeman. He is Julian Quist, who is a friend of your husband's."

"Oh, God!" the voice said.

"If you are Maureen Craven," Quist said quietly, "you can count on me to help in any way I can. If there are secrets to be kept, you will explain to me why and I will keep them. May I tell you that the wounded policeman you mentioned to Miss Connors on the phone is my closest friend. I am really here to help him, more than for any other reason."

"You were going to promote Bart's campaign, which I gather is over the hill," the voice said. Under the grating sound of it was a despair that was hard to take.

"If you are Maureen, let us in," Miss Connors said. "We can't help you standing out here in the hall, my dear."

The door closed, there was the sound of a chain being removed, and then it opened. Standing inside was a woman. She was slender, moderately tall, bright red hair, cut rather short. Her face was entirely covered by a black cloth mask. She gestured for them to come in. They went down a narrow little hall and found themselves in a small, cramped living room. If Maureen Craven lived here, Quist thought, it was rented furnished from someone with no taste at all.

"Please take that thing off, my dear," Miss Connors said.

The woman stood very still for a moment and then she raised her hands. "Brace yourselves," she said, and removed the black cloth mask.

Miss Connors screamed! Quist felt as if he'd been hit by a heavyweight in the pit of his stomach. He actually felt himself bending down, as if to protect himself from a second blow.

What the woman revealed was out of a horror film. Terribly scarred colorless tissue, one eyelid drooping in a gruesome comic wink, a mouth that seemed to be painted on around a dark hole. It was ghastly beyond description.

The woman put the cloth mask back in place. Miss Connors was choking back something like sobs. The thick, harsh voice was so bitter it seemed to lash at them.

"So you can't be any surer, can you, Nadine?"

Miss Connors moved unsteadily to a chair and sat down, covering her face with her hands. Quist found himself remembering the glamorous pictures tacked to the walls of George Strock's office. Could this possibly be the same woman?

"Yes, I am Maureen Craven, Mr. Quist," the woman said. "What is left of her! I suppose you've seen pictures of me?"

"Yes."

There was a hideous caricature of a laugh from behind the mask, hands raised to touch the black cloth. Quist found himself afraid she was going to remove it again. He didn't want that. He didn't want that very much.

"This is not like growing old," the rasping voice said.

"When you grow old I imagine you can see remnants of yourself, memories of yourself in what is there. But this is . . . nightmare!"

"Only an hour or two ago I was discussing with someone the possibility that you had, after all, been in a fire," Quist said.

"Not a possibility. A fact, Mr. Quist."

"The Fairmount?"

"Yes."

"And you were taken to St. Margaret's burn unit where Dr. Martine cared for you?"

"Cared for me!" Again that grinding laughter. "What a way to put it! Cared for me!"

"So he did know who you were?"

"Yes, yes, yes, he knew!"

"And waited seven years before deciding to tell Bart?"

"The money ran out," Maureen said. She had to be Maureen, Quist had decided.

He felt his muscles tighten. "And you went to his office and shot him?"

"No!" she cried out. "I wish to God I had!"

"Then it was Bart?"

"No!"

Quist felt a cold chill run down his spine. "Bart's known all along, hasn't he? This is where he comes when he disappears, isn't it? To see you, to care for you. Maybe to punish you?"

"No, no, *no!*" Her whole body seemed to writhe. "I haven't seen or heard from Bart since he went away to Teheran, seven years ago last August. I don't want to see him now. He mustn't know. That's why I asked Nadine for help. Because it said in the news he was looking for the killer. If he finds him he'll—he'll go like the others. Like your friend the policeman!" She turned away and was suddenly kneeling by Nadine Connor's chair. "My

187

dear, darling Nadine!" It was a gravel whisper. "Can you imagine how much I want to touch you, to be held in your arms, to cry there? But I know it would revolt you. Let me, at least, try to convince you that I am Maureen. That last time, when you were in New York, those few days. Do you remember what we talked about?"

"Of course," the old actress said, not taking her hands away from her face. She couldn't bear to look.

The black mask turned to Quist. "This is the secret, Mr. Quist, that I told Nadine that time, seven years ago. My—my marriage to Bart was not quite so perfect as the whole world thought. Oh, he was kind, tender, generous, loving. No woman could have asked for more, except for one thing."

"Children?" Quist said.

"You've been digging into my past, Mr. Quist. Yes, that was the flaw. We tried for medical help, Bart and I. The results were pretty awful for him. He was the reason. He was, God help him, sterile. The doctor tried various drugs, hormones, what have you. Nothing worked. The psychological effect on Bart was that he became impotent. He could no longer make love. He lived in a kind of perpetual shame. When Nadine came here that time, seven years ago, Bart and I had not been lovers for almost two years. I was frantic—pity for him, a terrible need and desire for myself. I told Nadine what my problem was, and she gave me advice." The mask turned back to the older woman. "Does that convince you, my darling? No one else on earth could know what I've just told you both. You did give me advice, didn't you?"

The old woman reached out, took Maureen in her arms, and held her. It was a long time before the quiet weeping subsided and Maureen turned back to Quist.

"The advice Nadine gave me was that . . ."

"That you take a lover," Quist said.

"I loved Bart so much but my need was so great, Mr. Quist. And the opportunity was there."

"Jack Milburn," Quist said.

Maureen scrambled up to her feet, her fists clenched at her side. "You are hearing things that can destroy lives, Mr. Quist," she said. "I knew I could trust Nadine, but I should never have let her bring you in here."

"Jack knows you're alive, living here?" he asked.

"No, no! He was convinced long ago that I died in the fire. Let me tell you, so that you can understand. Nadine had suggested that I take a lover, and Jack was suggesting the same thing. Not for the same reason. He didn't know about Bart. I was alone for a while, he was attracted to me. And I needed someone so very badly. I fought it off until two days before Bart was due home. And then I gave in, because I knew that once Bart was back it would have no permanence, it wouldn't go on. I was known in so many places. It couldn't happen at my apartment because of Rachel. It couldn't happen at Jack's apartment because Bart and I were in and out of there often. Our kind of hotel was dangerous. So Jack arranged for a room at the Fairmount. It was a dreadful place, cheap, tawdry, but what I needed so desperately was possible there. We spent an afternoon together and then—then we were both ravenously hungry! So Jack got up, dressed, and went out to get us some sandwiches and coffee at a neighborhood delicatessen. He never came back. Two or three minutes after he was gone the Fairmount was a raging furnace. They said—afterward —that it was arson. Someone had spread kerosene or gasoline in the hallways. It—it didn't start slowly, it started like an explosion. I was suddenly inside a wall of flames. I—oh my God—I knew I wasn't going to get out! I knew I was going to die. Maybe like drowning —you see a dozen images. It would destroy Bart if he knew I'd been in this place with a man. I remember fighting my way, naked, through flames to the bureau. My purse was there—credit cards, driver's license. I grabbed it up, threw it into the center of the flames and, I thought, died."

"Oh, my poor child!" Nadine Connors said.

"When I came to I was in an emergency area of the hospital. The pain was something you wouldn't believe. I couldn't see. I couldn't speak or cry out. It—it was worse than this." She pointed to her throat. "Days went by, and I could see that people flinched when they looked at me. I could see a little by then. There was a nurse who was kind and gentle. I asked her why everyone turned away when they looked at me. They kept my hands strapped to the side of the bed so I couldn't irritate the raw surfaces all over my body. This nurse must have thought that, brutal as it might be, it would be good therapy. She brought me a hand mirror. I looked in it and fainted."

"Oh, sweet Mother!" Miss Connors murmured.

"I don't know what's better," Maureen said. "To know the truth or to live with hope when there is no hope. This nurse—and I'm grateful to her now—believed in truth. She told me I'd had the best possible emergency care, the best people in the business, and the dice had come up sevens. I was going to have to learn to live with it."

"And Bart?" Quist asked.

"I never wanted him to see me. I didn't want pity. I didn't want him to know what had happened to me or how it had happened. I didn't want Jack Milburn to know I'd survived. He'd have felt obligated to me."

"That's when Dr. Martine became a part of your life?"

190

Maureen nodded. "He told me he wasn't going to be able to do much for me, but that I was going to survive—if that was important. Now I must get around to the business of telling them who I was. They'd found no identification to account for me. I—I played crazy for a while—pretended I didn't know, couldn't remember. All the time I was telling myself that Bart must never know. Better that I just disappear than for him to know that I'd betrayed him with another man. One thing was certain. No one was ever going to look at me and know that I was Maureen Tate, the film star, who had married Bartley J. Craven, the well-known diplomat. I was an unrecognizable piece of junk!

"But Dr. Martine had all the skills of a good physician, the bedside manner, the patient sympathy. I had to go somewhere to recuperate. Who were my friends? Where was my life? Perfectly legitimate questions for him to ask. I needed help. Finally I told him something. I was married. I'd been staying in the Fairmount with a lover. I had the money to take care of myself. I would rather die than have my husband know the truth."

"You had money of your own?" Quist asked.

"Quite a bit of money," Maureen said. "Bart never knew." The black mask turned to Nadine Connors. "I was sure Bart was forever, but just in case I was wrong, I wasn't going to be left on another doorstep."

"Mad money," Quist said, remembering the phrase.

"Dr. Martine seemed sympathetic. He kept asking me about how much money I had. He had to know what I could afford, didn't he?" Bitterness was back in the voice, if it could be called a voice. "We became co-conspirators. He provided me with the identity of a woman who'd died in the fire. She was an old-maid schoolteacher from the Midwest somewhere—Ellen

191

Smith. Would you believe that someone from the school where she worked came to see her, took one look at me, and got away as fast as he could? I could have been the remains of anyone! I got medical insurance and pension money from Ellen Smith.

"Dr. Martine finally moved me to an apartment, with a woman to come in and cook me a meal and straighten up for me. Then one day he let me have it. He knew who I was, or guessed who I was. I would now have to start to pay for his silence—but pay," Maureen said, taking a deep breath. "Until, at last, there was no more money. I pleaded with Martine to give me time to figure out a way. He wouldn't listen. Bart had money to keep on paying him for life. My friend went to see Martine, to plead with him I thought."

"What friend?"

"This friend, Julian," a voice from the doorway.

Quist spun around to find himself facing George Strock. The little detective's eyes looked like opaque marbles behind his wire-rimmed glasses. He was holding a very serviceable-looking handgun pointed straight at Quist's chest.

"You shouldn't have done it, my sweet," Strock said to Maureen. "You really shouldn't, you know. Now we're going to have to start stacking 'em up, like cordwood."

Strock had made his entrance without a sound, obviously he had a key. He had come down the little hallway while Maureen talked, any noise covered by that raucous voice.

Quist tried to play it cool, standing perfectly still. "We're here to help, not to hurt the lady, George," he said.

"Help or hurt, maybe the same thing," Strock said.

"I couldn't let you go on, George," Maureen said.

"One after another after another. I couldn't, for your own sake."

"You should have let me decide what I had to do, Maureen," Strock said.

"You turned out to be just as good as you've always said you were, George," Quist said, standing motionless. The gun was steady as a rock in Strock's hand. "How long ago did you find her?"

"Couple of years ago. Now don't come any closer, Maureen. I don't want to have to include you."

"Would you, George?" Maureen cried out. "Would you? It could be a way out!"

"Let's try to be sensible," Quist said. "How do you propose to hide stacks of bodies, George—like cordwood?"

"That won't really matter to you, Julian, will it?" Strock said. "You see, we've come a very long way to keep a secret, and, by God, we're going to keep it."

"Maureen doesn't want Bart to know," Quist said. "We'll keep her secret if she wants us to."

"Until you hit the pavement," Strock said, "and then you'll spread it like jam on a sandwich."

Quist gauged the distance between himself and the little detective with the gun. It would be three long strides, and while taking them, an expert with a gun, like Strock, could get off three or four shots. The only thing to do was stall for time—but time for what? Strock was obviously way off the rails, so, time for the mood to change, the whim to change.

"How did you come to find Maureen, George?" Quist asked. It was the right approach, he saw. It played on Strock's vanity.

"I'm a good detective, Julian. I've told you that. One of the best! Almost a year afterward I went back over the ground others had covered earlier. Sergeant Danforth of Missing Persons was a good man, but not as thorough as I am. With dental charts and medical records he proved that the unidentified woman from the Fairmount fire was *not* Maureen. I wondered if she could be one of the living, passing herself off as someone else, or mentally incompetent and wrongly identified as someone else. I saw half a dozen of the poor creatures. Like Maureen here, they'd have to convince you who they were with facts, with memories. You'd never know with what there was left to see. Well, the only one among the nine living survivors I wasn't able to check out was a schoolteacher named Ellen Smith from a small town in Ohio. Oh, the superintendent of schools for her district had gone to New York to see this Smith woman after the fire, but he was so shocked by what he saw that he got out of there as fast as he could. He arranged for pension funds, Medicare payments, to reach her at this address and then he tried to forget what he'd seen.

"So I came here to check out. Thorough, that's the George Strock trademark. In an hour I broke this phony Ellen Smith down. She was Maureen, the woman I'd been hired to find. She pleaded with me, begged me not to report back to my client. Nothing could be worse for him than to see her the way she is and be told how she happened to get that way. Desperate! So—so pathetically in need of help and understanding. She was right, of course. The truth would be worse for Craven than never having an answer."

"So you moved in here?" Quist asked.

"Not the way you're insinuating, you smirking bastard!" Strock said, his voice rising. For a moment Quist thought he had finished himself.

"He was a friend, a protector—a father to me," the

woman in the mask said. She raised a shaking hand toward that black covering. "Can you imagine anyone making love to this?"

There was a little choking sound from Nadine Connors.

"Every month there was money to pay to Martine," Strock said. "Maureen began to run out of what she'd saved, and I tried to find some in other places. But finally, this week, we couldn't meet the payment. I went to plead with him. The sonofabitch just laughed at me. Right while I stood there he picked up the phone and called Bart Craven. And so—I killed them both, him and his woman.

"I had to get out of there because I knew Bart was coming. I took Martine's keys and got out. I knew I'd have to come back because, somewhere, that blackmailing creep would have some record of Maureen, the truth about her. I couldn't get back in the house until the next night, but thanks to you and your friendship with Kreevich, I knew the police hadn't found anything yet. I searched and searched and in the middle of it that poor slob of a caretaker walked in. I had to shut him up."

"And Kreevich?"

"Nice guy, good guy. He needed my help so he talked freely to me. If Bart was telling the truth, then Martine must have some kind of file on Maureen. It wasn't in the house so he was going to the hospital to search Martine's records there. I couldn't go with him, but I followed him there. He wasn't in there too long—an hour, hour and a half. Then he came out in a hurry. In my business you get to sense things. I knew damn well he must have found something, was headed here. I couldn't risk it, so I just stepped in front of him and let him have it. I regretted it, Julian. That's the truth. He was a nice guy."

195

Quist's mouth was dry. This little man was mad as a hatter, he thought.

At that moment there was a sound of splintering wood from down the dark hall. Someone had broken in the front door. Strock turned, and in that moment Quist had him. He sprang forward, landing, literally, on the little detective's back. His right hand closed on Strock's gun arm and he beat it against the hardwood floor until he saw the gun slither a yard or so away. He raised up and brought the edge of his hand down in a chopping karate blow to the side of Strock's neck. Only then, as the body under him went limp, did he turn to see what had created the diversion that had clearly saved their lives.

He'd heard Maureen scream, and now he knew why. Standing facing her was her husband, Bart Craven. He held out his hands to his wife. "You shouldn't have, Maureen," he said gently. "You should have known I would have forgiven you. You should have known I'd have cared for you, loved you always. That I always will!"

And then Bart had his lost woman in his arms.

Quist, a knee in the small of George Strock's back, turned his head to the woman who sat frozen in an armchair. "Would you very much mind, Miss Connors, going to that phone in the corner and calling the police?"

"Don't ever tell me that some people don't have special powers," Quist said. He and Lydia were sitting together on the loveseat in front of a crackling fire on the hearth in their Beekman Place living room. "Bart had never believed from the first day that Maureen was dead. Something would have turned off inside him if she were gone. And it didn't."

"I wonder how he could be sure it wasn't just something he hoped for?"

"He was sure. In any case it kept him going. After the Martine business he was sure she was close by. He really did set out to look for the killer. This is a bright man, you know, who as a diplomat had dealt with the double-cross, the triple-cross, the always improbable. If Maureen were alive and in big trouble—and the murders suggested it—who would she turn to for help? There was just one person he could think of—Nadine Connors, her close friend and benefactor from way back. And so Bart started to camp on Miss Connors's trail."

"He saw us go to the theater to see her night before last?"

"Yes. And then he saw her come here this morning. He followed Miss Connors and me when we went downtown, saw us go into 81½. He was debating what to do when another actor came on stage. George Strock! What was going on? Friends, an employee he trusted, were hiding something from him. He went into the vestibule of 81½. No familiar names on the mailboxes. He rang a couple of bells till somebody let him in. He apologized, said he'd rung the wrong bell when somebody called down to him. Then he went from door to door, listening."

Lydia turned her head. "How could he hear you talking from out in the hall?"

"It's not like here, love," Quist said, "81½ Second Avenue is a jerry-built junk pile. He could hear. Strock's voice was familiar, my voice was familiar. And there was that awful voice he'd never heard, Maureen's. He never thought of anything but getting in there and he smashed his way in."

"And saved your life," Lydia said.

"And maybe his, and maybe hers," Quist said. "He's a man who really loves, and that may win for both of them."

"What did Strock have to gain?" Lydia asked. "I don't understand him. Was he forcing himself on Maureen? Was it some kind of perversion?"

"I don't think so," Quist said. "A kind of madness, if you like. Strange thing is he told me about it, when I first met him. The story of *Laura,* an old book and movie, about a detective who falls in love with the portrait of a woman who's presumed to be dead. And then she turns up. Strock found Maureen, after dreaming about her, and she was his to keep, to protect, to love in his own confused way."

"How awful for her!"

"I think not. She was more alone than anyone you can imagine. I think she was grateful to him, until he went on a killing binge."

They sat staring into the fire for a moment.

"What about Kreevich?" Lydia asked.

Quist smiled at her. "Maybe I've got Bart's disease," he said. "But I'm certain he's going to make it."